THE
AMETHYST
GUARDIAN

THE AMETHYST GUARDIAN

Helena Carmichael

ISBN-13: 978-0-645829-60-0

Connell Publishing

connellpublishing.com.au

PROLOGUE

E ons ago, the people from Earth had come to The New World. They had been carefully chosen for the brilliance of their minds and the skill of their hands. To build a new civilization on a pristine turquoise planet. A civilization unlike any other. At one with nature or contained in compact cities on a single continent.

Despite its looks, unfortunately, the planet they had chosen was not the wilderness they had imagined it to be. It was an abandoned battlefield of once powerful forces. Aggressive invaders from the stars, the Saurians, had been met by the citizens of Homeland in a war that had changed parts of the New World forever, before the enemy had been forced deep underground. Most of the population had been slaughtered. Those who remained had gathered in the foothills of Far Mountain and had allowed nature to reclaim the ruins of their civilization. It was agreed to look forward, and let the past fear and tragedy fade.

Only a few Guardians would continue to keep the records safe and even fewer, the Dark Guardians, were trained to protect and maintain vigilance from the shadows. A remnant of the old age, a gossamer web, formed an ancient planetary defence system. It was all but invisible and only activated in the presence of weapons so the peaceful newcomers passed through it unharmed.

Homeland's inhabitants feared the worst when the Earthers arrived, but were pleasantly surprised by the depth of character and intelligence the newcomers displayed. The Elders approved of the settler's plans to contain the new civilization and to prevent the mistakes of their past. Both peoples were human, their languages different, but in time combined to a single dialect as the loneliness of being the last survivors faded into a new, stable world order.

The Far Mountain people lived in harmonious small towns, dressed as their ancestors had done, enjoyed the simple pleasures of farming and craft whereas the New Worlders built five vertical, contained cities nestled in untouched wilderness on an abandoned continent that were as unnatural they were filled with science, art and culture. Forests and vast plains were left untouched, slowly swallowing the carved stone remnants of the ancient world.

Trade and travel between the two continents were allowed and anyone who wanted to holiday in the other land was welcomed with open arms, but closer contact was rare. Not exactly forbidden, but frowned upon. Luckily few citizens of the New World could stand the prolonged tranquillity of a low-tech life and even fewer Far Mountainers could bear the excitement of Harbour City. The hard lines of the architecture and the greyness of the clothing everyone wore reminded them somewhat of the enemy that had almost destroyed them.

It was a peaceful coexistence on a peaceful planet. Animals and plants flourished as orange sunshine bathed the clean waters surrounding the towns and cities. Only occasionally a Sky Train would connect the two peoples across the ocean. Harmony reined.

But, deep underground, the dormant evil ones were awakening. Forced into subterranean chambers, but not exterminated, the enemy multiplied, and planned. This time there would be no opposition to the Saurians. By the time they were ready, their prey would have become so weak from disease, they would scarcely find the means to fight. This time, victory would be assured. Focussed on the symptoms of a deadly plague, no one in New Homeland even noticed that the war had already begun. No one but Elyse.

CHAPTER 1

Elyse.

The Sky Train whirred to a halt at Harbour City Central station and the doors slid open, triggering lights that turned standby dimness into an overpowering bright glow. A line of black uniformed, faceless health security personnel waited at their designated Decon Portals, ready to protect the many workers within the silver transport. This was the only time people were allowed to come into such close contact. It was an economic necessity.

The sparkling, white perfection of the platform rose up to greet her sensible low-heeled shoes while Elyse clutched her portfolio and pressed it tightly against her side as an endless grey sea of commuters washed to either side of her, flowing towards the tunnels on their way to work where they would industriously spend the day, before once more catching the Sky Train.

She hesitated momentarily looking down at the black crystal landing pad before stepping onto the wet platform. The air was crisp with morning chill. Over the sound of footsteps, voices and the pressure hose constantly cleaning, disinfecting and dissolving any microscopic particles, she could hear the haunting sound of a flute, far below in the tunnels. The vaguely familiar melody was beautiful, lilting between major and minor keys and resolving into perfection.

Even as the musician in her hummed in tune with the flute, attempting to pin it down in her memory. She was sure she had played this tune more than once. The scientific part of her brain observed the crowd funnelling and thickening as workers jostled each other for position to enter the portals which sprayed an invisible dry mist onto their bodies and left them looking an ever-paler grey.

As her turn to be decontaminated approached, she swallowed hard and adjusted her filter mouthpiece slightly. Not even holding her breath could exclude the bitter droplets that stung like a thousand microscopic needles wherever they touched. Acceptance was the only option. She nodded, giving a heartfelt silent thankyou to the health security person, knowing they were at the front line of this world-wide battle for survival against a species they could not even see.

A species that had hidden its DNA and advanced at an incredible rate across the globe, infecting both humans and animals and turning them into pained, misshapen husks of their former selves. After eating through skin and muscle, the organism sometimes moved into a person's central nervous system, switching impulses off, until movement slowed and stopped, followed by the inevitable decline into coma and death. It had evaded any and all the technology and chemicals thrown at it and had grown ever stronger.

Involuntarily, her hand touched the still tingling and tender patch on her forearm as she removed her mouthpiece. If she hadn't been infected then she would never have been desperate enough to search the ancient herbal archives for an answer. She would still have been floundering in new technology like everyone else. And if she hadn't been infected, she would not have had a live sample of the species living comfortably on her arm. Not a mindless virus as it appeared when viewed in its dead and dehydrated state.

Elyse had carefully shaved a sliver of infected tissue from her own arm and peered at it under her high-powered viewer. What had appeared was as shocking as it was unexpected. Tiny but evil lizard-like animals, greyish with wrinkled shiny skins, that moved with purpose and intent. Walking on their two hind legs and using their shorter front legs like arms they looked almost alien. Unlike anything she had ever seen. They cut and carried her cells, only to deposit them in ringed walls where more of the microscopic creatures sheltered and multiplied.

Elyse had jerked back from the viewer in shock, then peered at them once move. Oblivious to her gaze, the microscopic creatures carried on their lives. Quickly, she had run to her freezer where the dehydrated herbal extracts she had ready for testing were stored. She drew up a tiny sample and squirted it onto the creatures. Nothing happened with the first or second samples, the third however caused the creatures to scurry madly and erratically, then, as one, collapse and turn to grey, powdery dust. And, instantaneously, the itch in her arm stopped. Without hesitation, she shaved the adjacent sliver of tissue and studied it. The creatures were nowhere to be seen. Only the same powdery residue remained. She carefully scooped it up into a sterile tube and capped it before storing it back in the freezer. One day she would have the time to study it in depth.

Letting out a deep sigh of relief and satisfaction, Elyse knew the direction her life had to take from that moment on. The herbal archive contained long since desiccated and frozen specimens from this new world. Some were contaminated with something not able to be identified.

Some sort of organic substance. She had to somehow find the original plants, if they still even existed and she had to reproduce their properties in large enough quantities to be able to stop the diminutive invasion. For now, she had to rely on modern technology, nonspecific poisons, cleanliness and distance from personal interactions to prevent another attack on her tissues.

Elyse rubbed the tender patch again before being pulled her out of her reverie by someone pushing past her. She shrank from the unexpected contact at the same time as a sign over her head blazed on with a "No touching!" command. Her crowd discomfort magnified until it was almost unbearable.

The bitterness of the decon spray subsided and the stinging diminished as she was washed towards the platform exit.

Breathing deeply, she entered the steep, roughly hewn, dark tunnel leading to the street. The daily contrast of the tunnel, an incongruous remnant of the old city and the clinically bright platform never seemed to diminish. Unconsciously slowing, Elyse joined the stragglers bringing up the rear. Were they all as scared of crowds, and tunnels and trains as she was? Probably not. A tiny shot of panic shot across her forehead as the tunnel closed in, just as it did every morning but the flute music swirled around her today, encouraging her to keep heading into the dimness. She had to know where it was coming from.

Watery, early morning sunlight beaconed the commuters. As they diverged and hurried away, Elyse saw him. The musician. He sat cross-legged against the green tiled wall, seemingly oblivious to the world around him.

Lost in the beauty the man was creating, Elyse forgot her own need for haste and stepped out of the stream of workers towards him. He was simply gorgeous. She could see it despite the long hair that fell across one eyebrow and the beard that shaded his face as he blew across the flute, allowing exquisite notes to escape. His fingers were long and moved with a practiced precision that belied the depths to which he had fallen. He belonged in a concert hall, surrounded by an audience of glittering admirers, not sitting here alone on the cold ground.

She held her breath as she edged closer and sheltered against the wall, allowing herself to simply stop and enjoy the final strains of the song.

"Funeral for the world?" She whispered as she crouched down and carefully placed some money into his flute case. It didn't look like he was having a very profitable morning. Not many people could appreciate the intricate beauty of the Far Mountain composer's saddest song.

He nodded, looking over her left shoulder and smiled slightly, before lifting the flute once more. His eyes were dark and unfocused. Elyse peered into them, willing a response even as she realized he couldn't see her. An involuntary pang of sadness touched her before she could stifle it. She straightened and turned away even as some primitive emotion deep within urged her to stay by his side. He was playing again, oblivious to her reactions. Another Far Mountain song. A happy one this time. Even as she waited for elevator in her office building, she was still humming the tune.

CHAPTER 2

Adrian watched the slight woman walking away and felt an annoying little itch between his shoulder blades. Every time he saw her, small details of her personality emerged until he had become completely mesmerised by her quiet shy charm. She was beautiful, with soft, serene features, but perhaps too introverted to attract a normal male. It was like she was a treasure that only he could see. The thought made him a little glad.

As she had emerged from the tunnel, she had looked hesitant, almost afraid. He started playing her favourite song when he heard the Sky Train arriving. Perhaps he should have been more careful, avoided contact. But he hated how uncomfortable she was every morning. Distracting her had worked. She walked with purpose now, her heels striking the pavement in time to his song. She could probably dance, he thought absently. How much would he love to drop all pretence and just fly to her, scoop her in his arms and take off for the sky. They could dance through the glowing sunset clouds and glide into the evening stars. Instead, he sat here, in the dirt and longed for her.

Lost in his fantasy he almost missed the shadowy figure that detached itself from the crowd and steered into a close formation behind the woman like an evil shadow as she disappeared around a corner. A dank chill moved with the shadow and dread wrapped its tendrils around Adrian's throat. He swallowed and stood fluidly, as he brushed his hair back, shedding his tattered cloak to reveal a business suit which almost instantly transformed him into yet another ordinary office worker. His flute, folded swiftly into a briefcase, added to the illusion.

He had to move quickly to catch up to the pair. The woman had almost reached her office tower, her skirt swished around her slim ankles and her long, pale hair swung ever so slightly from side to side as she took each step. That meant she was hurrying. He knew why. The man behind her took longer, slower steps while keeping an exact distance from her. He was impossibly thin, even in a suit similar to Adrian's and he sported a short back and sides in the latest fashion of the city folk. No one gave him a second glance.

Adrian increased his speed until he was within arm's length of his quarry. Just as the man crouched, ready for a sprint to intercept Elyse before she left the sidewalk, Adrian lunged, grasped the man's shoulder and dragged him into a side alley. He had to make sure. The man hid behind very dark sunglasses. Adrian smiled and tapped the him on the shoulder as if they were old friends then as he pulled his hand back, he knocked the sunglasses from the man's face. The eyes were unmistakeable. Pale yellow, with a vertical sliver of pupil showing, almost reptilian eyes, set in a grey wrinkled skin. It was a Saurian.

The yellow eyes narrowed as the Saurian in turn recognised Adrian and the alien's left arm reached across his back and into his right pocket. Emerging with a curved knife the arm twisted and lengthened as it grew to twice its length. Adrian had to duck as the Saurian swung the knife but he was ready for the move, blocking, then grasping the cold wrist and twisting it forcefully, using the Saurians momentum against him. The hand still holding the knife could do little to prevent the fatal plunge into its owner's stomach.

A foul stench emanated from the wound as roiling greyness oozed out and puddled on the concrete beneath. As it hit the disinfected ground, the greyness seethed and jerked and then was still. Adrian watched until the pale eyes lost focus and the narrow pupils dilated into huge empty discs, then set the body carefully against the wall. Within seconds the entire thing had dissolved into the concrete and then continued sinking until it was out of sight. Back from where it had emerged.

A slight sadness touched Adrian at the thought of another life lost, even one as evil as this one. Another death to add to his ledger. Another weight for his soul to bear. But he had no choice. Once Elyse had been targeted, these monsters would not stop. Her work was too important to endanger. Not only for his people, but for the entire world.

A small voice in his head argued that it wasn't her work he was protecting. Maybe at first that's all it had been. But now all he could think about was keeping her safe, keeping her close, even though they could never have a future. Dark Guardians were destined to be alone. He had to stifle the feelings that continued to interfere with the single mindedness his role entailed.

Turning his palm over to expose a metallic black cuff around his wrist, he dialled in the kill. He didn't enjoy it, but he took his role very seriously. He hoped this creature was the only one following her, but he doubted it.

AJH

CHAPTER 3

The frenetic, almost panicked pace of the lab crowded out any thoughts of music. Elyse hurriedly removed her cloak and scarf and opened her portfolio. Feathery pencil drawings of alpine herbs spilled out over her desk, interspersed with pages of organic chemistry equations. Even after five years of research, the sight of medicinal plants still filled her with excitement. The future was here, lying on her desk, waiting to be released.

The next step would be even more exciting. Maybe even a little terrifying. She had to climb a mountain, literally, to collect more samples. She'd been relying on dehydrated specimens from the university vault and even with those, her results were outstanding. She was hoping that doing her next series of experiments at altitude, with fresh plant material would take things to a new level.

Maybe ancient herbal wisdom could succeed where technology was failing. Alpine plants eked out a living in the most inhospitable places on the turquoise planet. Barely enough rocky soil to sink their cobwebby roots into, they endured intense solar radiation by day and froze each night. Their cells would become solid, bristling with icicles. With the rising sun they would defrost and live again. It was this cyclic freeze and thaw that might hold the answers she was looking for.

But there was a missing link – the organic residue. Elyse needed to find out what it was.

As always, the spectre of the plague tearing across the world and leaving people and animals twisted in torturous agony hung over her and overlay the happiness that her work brought her.

It was only here, in the laboratory, surrounded by like-minded scientists who had long since become both friends and the family she never had, was Elyse able to shed her crippling shyness.

Without revealing that she herself had been infected, as that would have meant immediate suspension and isolation, Elyse had proposed her theory to her team leader at their weekly meeting. Her colleagues were both intrigued and supportive, adding some good suggestions as to other plants that could be studied for similar effects. A new research direction had formed.

Their excitement overflowed into lunches where they would discuss their new and developing project. Her lab of biologists was part of a five-city wide team of scientists working on a solution, from chemists to engineers, mathematicians to epidemiologists. It was an amazing group of people and when they met on Vis-comm system gatherings, and the room would fill with their bioluminescent holographic images, she could only marvel at the tiny fragment her own work brought to this jigsaw puzzle of a cure.

After writing a proposal that took weeks and several revisions, both by herself and her team leader, her project had been accepted by the Council of Infection Research and she had received funding to travel to Far Mountain to collect samples of the fresh alpine plant she sought.

An entire day spent packing fragile test tubes and pipettes, scalpels and solutions into her purpose-built backpack meant she was ready for home. Her heartbeat quickened in anticipation, thinking of the musician from this morning. She looked for him on her way to the tunnel but the wall was blank and silent. It felt as if he had been only a dream man because no one could have been so perfectly designed and real at the same time. How sad was it that he couldn't see? Was that why he was a busker? Was he homeless? What was he doing right now? Elyse gave herself up to thoughts only of him until the train gently descended before gliding to her stop.

Home was a tiny 20th floor apartment with a view of the lights of the city. Without the view it would have been almost unbearably cramped but the floor to ceiling wall of windows invited the whole world to be part of her life. Potted trees and shrubs framed the view and filled her space with happy life. Elyse sighed with contentment as she carefully deposited the backpack on her diminutive coffee table and sank into the couch. While she was at work she loved to talk and laugh and interact with her fellow scientists, looking almost confident but afterwards she craved silence and the comfort of being alone. The couch was possibly her favourite place in the whole of New World.

Her winter hiking clothes were already tucked into a larger backpack that neatly hid her work pack so she was basically ready for the long-haul Sky Train across the emerald ocean to New Homeland in the morning. Just a second to relax, she thought dreamily before drifting off into a gentle slumber, the sightless dark eyes of her dream man watching over her like a guardian angel.

CHAPTER 4

The fresh air of Homeland in the springtime caressed Elyse's cheek with its cool touch. She took a reflexive deep breath of happiness, feeling the refreshing breeze rush into her lungs. It was like having a drink of pure spring water. Her eyes drank in the sunshine and natural beauty around her. Trees swayed gently in the breeze and flowering shrubs glistened in the shimmering light.

If she had turned around, her exuberant mood would have turned to fear as an impossibly slim female figure with close cut spiky hair detached from the train behind her and followed menacingly. The evil of the city had shadowed her here.

The silver Sky Train left the open-air station and whirred away into the blue-green distance. Elyse turned, backpack slung over one shoulder to make her way from the platform, across the station and onto the street below. How different was this sunlit, open journey from the claustrophobic tunnel of the Sky Trains of Harbour city. Before long she was traversing the cobbled main street of the tiny town, nestled in the foothills of the massive snow-capped bulk of Far Mountain.

Finding the inn was almost too easy and after dropping off her equipment and freshening up, Elyse set off for the only café in town. It was almost too pretty for words, festooned with tiny lights strung through hanging baskets of colourful alpine flowers. It felt like home for a botanist. She couldn't help running her fingers lightly over their nodding heads as she entered the café and waited for her eyes to adjust to the peaceful dimness within. The interior didn't disappoint either. Deep mauves, blues and greens gave it a jewel like feeling and offset the bunches of deep pink flowers on the metallic, marble tables. A gleaming state of the art coffee machine took centre stage. The best of old Earth, right here in the furthest reaches of the New World.

A glowing pastry display case made her realise just how hungry she was. Beyond hungry. Several groups of people sat here and there murmuring softly and piano music drifted across the room. Only one man sat alone, in the corner with his back to the wall, hunched under a low cap, with only his strong jaw showing, cradling a cup of coffee. Even from across the room, she saw how the traditional shirt stretched across his broad shoulders. He didn't quite fit into this relaxed and pretty space. He needed open air and freedom. Elyse smiled to herself. Her imagination was getting away from her.

Stepping up to the counter she smiled at the barista even as a gentle wave of recognition echoed deep in her subconscious. He was an older man, distinguished and handsome. Tall and strong looking with a shock of silver hair. She had to look up to see his eyes and was surprised at the intensity with which he looked at her. For a long second, he didn't smile, but just seemed to look into her soul before his eyes brightened and his face broke into a welcoming, fatherly grin.

"What's good?" she ventured. "It's been a really long road to get here!"

His smile widened and, the earlier scrutiny forgotten, he seemed to be trying to put her at ease. "Can't go past the Sweetberry pie. Made it myself this morning. And my coffee isn't half bad either."

"Thanks, that sounds wonderful," Elyse smiled back, feeling her initial disquiet fade into a warm glow of happiness. She took a seat looking out over the main street, framed by flowers and the glow increased as she tasted the smooth dark berries in the crumbly light crust and turned into mellow contentment as she sat back and sipped her coffee. This place was pure magic. Maybe she could stay here forever and become part of the wing-backed chair she sat in. Work could wait, couldn't it? She found herself humming Funeral for the World and thinking of the blind musician. She felt close to him even though there was an ocean between them.

Absentmindedly, she looked around the coffee shop and locked eyes with the man in the corner. He had been staring at her from across the room but quickly looked down again as soon as she noticed. Not before recognition struck again. Not a gentle wave this time, but a strong jolt straight to her heart. She knew this man too? Had they met before? In a previous life maybe. Did he feel it too? What was going on here on the far side of the world? Elyse rubbed the side of her cup gently, willing the relaxed happiness of just doing nothing to return and in a small part it did, as long as she didn't look across the room.

Too soon it was over though, the empty coffee cup reproached her for even thinking of not continuing her work. Her research was potentially vital to the survival of almost everyone on the planet. She had to turn in early in preparation for an even earlier start up into the mountains. For several minutes she contemplated just staying here, peacefully idle, in this quiet little town where no parasites had yet shown. But nowhere on this world was completely safe, and would never be, if she failed in her quest.

It took some mental effort, but she made herself stand up and walk self-consciously past the man in the corner as she left. She waved briefly at his bowed head. He only nodded, keeping his head down but she felt him look up as she moved past. The intensity of his gaze burned even as she walked back towards the inn. The impulse to turn around and look back at him was overpowering and she had to bite her lip and hunch her shoulders to keep moving.   How strange these random emotions were.

CHAPTER 5

Had she glanced back, she would have seen him exhale for the first time. It had taken quite some effort to arrive before her and to position himself in her path for an accidental meeting. Now, once again, he saw her walk away from him without knowing how closely connected they were.

How would she react if and when she found out? Could she accept him for who he was? Or would she be horrified, as the world she recognised, tipped on its axis. Everything she knew as real would be stripped back to an older, more marvellous existence where Guardians served coffee and evil men tried to prevent the saviour of the world from following her destiny and completing her quest.

At least here, he would be able to see them coming and intercept them before they could get to the slight girl with the enormous brain. She really was the Guardian in this narrative, the only hope humanity had. Her road was fast becoming more treacherous and it wasn't just the inhospitable mountain terrain ahead that he worried about.

More customers wandered in and Adrian stood up and stretched himself to his full height. He was relieved to be home in the mountains where everyone was a friend and the air was free and fresh.

Harbour City had become a grey prison full of lifeless workers who knew neither friendship nor freedom. No wonder the parasites had full reign there. How long would it be before they were defeated, and how long, if ever, would it take for the truth to be uncovered? That the parasites were not a natural enemy but one that had been called from the depths of evil for an agenda too terrifying to contemplate. They had attacked with speed and precision. Everywhere throughout the five cities and at the same time, emerging from the depths, carried in the blood of the evil ones and transferred to their prey.

Long ago there had been a similar outbreak, when only the evil ones and the Guardians existed. The Guardians were driven further and further up into the mountains to starve or freeze. Instead, they had found salvation, in the form of tiny alpine plants, which froze at dusk and thawed as the sun's rays touched their feathery fronds. Even as the weary defenders found shelter deep in the mountain caves and sustenance in the plants, they grew strong and resilient, so when the evil ones finally arrived, they were no match for the Guardians. Retreating into their cavernous subterranean lair, they had stayed hidden until they were summoned to once again decimate the new population.

How was it that this insignificant looking Earther girl had independently found the Guardian's salvation? And she had not broadcast her findings like so many would have, for momentary fame and glory, but kept searching for answers and evidence. He could barely believe, that with no help from the Guardians themselves, she had found her way to his homeland and was even now preparing to climb the mountain by herself.

His pocket buzzed insistently and he placed his hand on his communicator. The others were ready. He smiled, thinking of how much he had missed his kinfolk and how reassuring it would be to see them again. Unconsciously, his steps quickened as he strode towards the meeting place where they waited for news from Harbour City of the New World.

CHAPTER 6

E lyse sat on the comfortable and incredibly soft bed with her growing tubes spread out before her. She checked the integrity of each. The glass was flawless and the growing medium fresh and waiting for the specimens she would hopefully be collecting tomorrow. Ten altogether. She hoped it would be enough. These plants were so precious, so rare and so powerful that she did not want to damage their ecosystem in any way. She wiped her scalpel, scraper and trowel with pure disinfectant solution and watched as the rainbow of evaporation flared and then disappeared from the surfaces of the tools. Carefully, she repacked them into her back pack along with provisions. No changes of clothes, toiletries or mementos.

She had been single-minded in her quest. Unable to travel because of the constant demands of her work, she had nevertheless gained mountaineering experience in the recreational holo-chambers at the sports club. She had endured and eventually enjoyed howling winds, freezing temperatures and climbing. So much climbing. Knowing she was ultimately safe made the experience exhilarating and she could not keep her excitement fully contained. She would have trouble sleeping tonight and every bit of preparation today would make her trek tomorrow less daunting.

Her outerwear was waterproof, the inner layers moisture wicking. She hoped against hope that the forecast sunny, crisp weather would hold. It was a mountain after all. It made its own weather – so often a ring of foggy ice storms was photographed near the summit. She didn't have to climb all the way up. Nothing grew there, the rocks were glassy and hard, the terrain inhospitable. Not many people had conquered this mountain. More had died in the attempt than had succeeded. It wasn't the highest peak on the planet, just the one furthest away from Harbour city and most city folk didn't see the point of climbing it when the chances of returning were so slim.

Just for a brief moment she regretted coming here without telling anyone bar her team leader the exact location. Her reasons were sound. The fewer people that knew about her research, the smaller the risk that it would be confiscated by the big companies to get lost in the many unfinished projects lying abandoned and dusty on their shelves.

CHAPTER 7

The small, antique carved wooden door opening onto the cobbled street belied the large courtyard garden within and the even larger meeting hall beyond. Arching trees were underplanted with herbs spilling over raised garden beds that surrounded an intricate fountain and gave the whole garden an almost magical feel. Adrian had to duck to pass under the lintel and smiled as the familiar sound of his friends already arguing amicably carried over the bubbling of the fountain. He unstrapped his side arm and unclicked his cuff before tossing them into the waiting basket along with the others and stepped up to meet his kin.

A hush came over the gathering as he walked in and he straightened unconsciously, wishing his brothers were beside him. It wasn't often that a Dark Guardian came home to his clan. They carried on their work largely alone in the New World. Their work was dangerous and violent, so at odds with the society here. These were the people Adrian protected from a distance, his people.

The silence lasted for long seconds as everyone drank in the sight of his strong silhouette in the doorway and then broke into a crescendo of happy greetings. He was surrounded by men and women, plainly dressed in pale linens who hugged him and patted him on the back. He felt tension dissolving as waves of friendship washed over him. Walking through the crowd he made his way to the pedestal in the centre of the room, lit by a vivid dome above. He stepped onto the stone platform and raised his arms over his head towards the light. It bathed him in glorious rainbows of colour and cleansed the grey ooze of the beasts he had slain from his soul. Everyone sang a simple harmony so the sound and the light mingled in the air.

The cleansing felt so good that he could have stayed there for the longest time, but he needed to let them know what had happened in the world, warn of the horror that approached and prepare them for the battle to come. He had not seen his friends before the cleansing, but now they surrounded him with good natured humour and camaraderie. He felt their youth and innocence, things he had lost in the city. Being a Dark Guardian came at a cost.

Thumping Adrian's back until his wings ached, and joking about his having a girlfriend, they once again made him feel part of a world that was strong and bright.

It was time to face the elders, the entire council had gathered today. As if choreographed to perfection, the crowd moved in unison to form concentric circles surrounding Adrian in the centre of the room.

He cleared his throat and launched into an account of his travels in New Homeland and Harbour City. The devastation that had befallen the New World. His discovery of a lone scientist who had followed the most tenuous of leads to their secret. Her character and qualities of discretion, precision and courage. He tried not to make his report too glowing, or too personal but that was close to impossible. She, frankly, was amazing and it was difficult not to shout her praises at the top of his lungs.

Quietness had fallen over the gathering when he had started talking, but as he paused, murmuring turned into sounds of wonder, fear, anger and resignation. His speech had polarised his kinfolk. Usually unanimous in their beliefs, they could not stay divided for long. He knew it would be a difficult road ahead, as did everyone else but it was a road they would travel together.

The discussion lasted for a long time. Resignation won. They would not help Elyse, but they would not hinder her either. Adrian would continue to watch over her from a distance and make sure she left Homeland as soon as she had gathered her specimens.

Breathing more easily after everyone but his friends had left, he was more than happy to spend an evening in their company. To be able to relax over an ale and just empty his mind of the terrible things he had seen and done would be almost possible here, but he doubted it.

CHAPTER 8

Air entered her lungs with biting clarity and came out in little puffs of steam as she pushed further up the mountain path. Elyse picked her way carefully around the tiny alpine plants so as not to disturb any of them. Now and then she stooped to gently brush the ice crystals from the furry grey leaves of this plant or that to take a closer look.

With a cliff beside her and a delicate yet hardy seasonal grass covered rise ahead, the mountain was showing her its best side. Elyse tried not to think of how narrow the grassy verge was, and how close to the edge of the precipice she was. Since childhood, she had always loved climbing up things – trees, hills, rock walls, but not so much coming down again. Her holo-chamber practice should have helped, but a quiver of vertigo threatened to derail the sheer joy of adventure.

It wasn't an idle search. The herb she was looking for was similar to many others, all adapting to the hostile environment with a coating of fuzzy hairs.

If she hadn't been looking quite so intently, she probably would have missed it. A rainbow glint in the sunshine, half hidden in a mound of orange, lichen covered rocks caught her eye. The most beautiful alpine plant she had ever seen. Ever widening circles of iridescent arrow shaped leaves in a perfect marriage of mathematics and art. A tiny branch of pure white flowers waved in the gentle mountain breeze from the centre of the plant. This was it!

Elyse slipped off her backpack and carefully placed it to the side before subsiding gratefully to the ground beside this incredibly rare and precious plant. For long moments she just gazed at it, silently thanking it for surviving the eons to be here in time to hopefully save the entire population of this planet. Then she turned to her bag and withdrew her macro viewer. The plant looked even more incredible through the lens. Each leaf was a work of art, fine deep green striations marked the veins through the multicolour iridescence. Tiny holes perforated the leaves here and there. The hairs looked like elongated diamonds reflecting the sparkle. The small flowers were multi petalled like a bunch of miniature fairy peonies.

"Wow," Elise whispered reverently. "You certainly look better than your poor cousins in my lab." The weirdness of talking to a plant was not lost on her, and she smiled. It was time to go to work. Stashing the lens, she pulled out her portable lab essentials. Growing tubes with tissue culture reagent gel, sterilized long handled tweezers, scalpels and scissors lay side by side in a felt roll. Suddenly Elise felt nervous even though this is what she had been born for and this was what she had trained for years to do.

Kneeling over the plant, she worked slowly and methodically, detaching ten leaves from the herb at the base of their stems and embedding them in the gel before pressing the lids tightly over the tubes. Using a stronger lens, she examined the last leaf more closely. The small holes were irregularly shaped, as if a tiny insect had chewed on them with sharp little teeth. That was unexpected, because her lab specimens had crumbled beyond this level of detail. After stowing them in her back pack she allowed herself to sink to the ground, threading her fingers absently through the fine grass. The plant didn't look too fazed by the plunder with barely a leaf out of place. Able to keep growing free in this beautiful mountainous wilderness.

As she sat quietly in the wintery sunshine, something moved suddenly beside her plant. Elyse held her breath and froze. Yes! The thing she had suspected. An insect. It jumped out of the grass and onto one of the remaining leaves. Before long it was chewing industriously.

Was this her missing link? Probably freezing and thawing each night along with the plant, it could literally die and come back to life over and over again. Did this tiny creature leave some of its microbiome on the plant? She would not harm the insect. Taking it out of its habitat would surely kill it and she knew it had to be a rare and important creature. Easing out her macro viewer again she gazed at it intently. It was the most beautiful grasshopper she had ever seen. Iridescent, like the plant, but purple with long legs for hopping, a head like a miniature deer, feathery winglets and multi-pronged antlers. Magical, almost.

It turned its head and she could have sworn it looked at her with comprehension, before jumping abruptly out of sight. How strange! A problem for another time. She was so tired. Elyse sighed again and relaxed back onto the grass.

Her fingertips touched something unexpected, something that shouldn't have been up here. Metal, unexpectedly warmer than its surroundings, intricate, about the size of her hand with a double loop at the back. It was half buried in the white rocky ground and intertwined with grass. Awake again, she tugged and clawed under its irregular edges until the mountain gave up its prize. It was a clasp, an amulet perhaps. A symbol of a time long ago before this age. The design was obscured by eons of pale glacial dirt. Power seemed to emanate from its jewelled core.

With no conscious thought, she knew she had to protect this precious object so she tucked it reverently into the inner pocket of her snow jacket. Gentle warmth emanated from it like an infrared glow. She felt almost comfortable in this alpine environment. Surely, she could sit here for just a little longer. Time enough to save the world later. Resting against a rock, Elyse sighed deeply and began to drift away.

CHAPTER 9

Before she had even registered a sound, Elise felt a deep vibration under her palms. Her sleepiness vanished. The stillness was being disturbed, but by what? Not a ground shiver, it was too regular a pulse. Then she heard it, the deep bass of sky motors shredding the thin mountain air. Without any clear reason, fear gripped and her heart began to beat ever so quickly as adrenalin flooded into her bloodstream. She hoped it was a sight-seeing flight and tried to prepare a friendly smile.

But then she saw it come into view over the rise behind her, flying nose down with singular intent, black and smoothed of all distinguishing features, all hopeful thoughts were extinguished in a burst of pure panic. It was the same arrow shape as the old Earth war machines. Built to attack. As it saw her the nose of the Sky-flyer edged up and it jagged around her, the pilot invisible behind a darkened windshield, the airframe bristling with armaments. Weapons were outlawed in the New World. Elyse kept the now thoroughly fake smile plastered on her face even as the scar on her arm tingled with foreboding. All alone. How could she have been so stupid?

The Sky-flyer circled around in unnatural darting motions until it was between her and the way back over the rise. Nothing but some slippery grass and a few rounded rocks to stop her tumbling over the edge to her death. The mild light-headedness she'd been feeling now threatened to overwhelm her and Elyse gave up the pretence of smiling as she tried to peer through the windshield of the flyer.

As if aware of her realization, tiny turrets opened under the fuselage and multiple grey streams of photons spurted on either side of her. She knew how much they would burn if they touched her skin. She had seen pictures of the wounded after the last war on Earth.

She only had two choices, stay and be burnt alive or jump. If she jumped, she could protect her precious cargo. Her notes were in her back pack. Someone would find them and send them back to her lab. Her team could complete her work.

In other words, no choice at all.

Taking a giant breath, she raced to the edge of the cliff pursued ever so much nearer by the flyer. Wind whipped her face with an incredible force, as if to push her back towards safety. She saw the bluest of mountains, embroidered with white snow, then the tree line and as she made it to the edge, the valleys and rivers and township. She marvelled in the beauty of it all even as her grief at dying misted her eyes.

Then, without hesitation, she leapt off the cliff into nothingness, gasping with the finality of what she had done.

And then she saw something else, someone else, rising up to meet her in the nothingness of wind and fall.

CHAPTER 10

I t was him.

Her blind musician, but he wasn't blind. His eyes weren't dark and unfocused any more, they were deep brown, shot through with vivid purple. It was also the man in the coffee shop, but not hidden under a cap. His dark hair shone and whipped back in the wind that lifted the cape around his shoulders. He held out his arms and caught her mid fall. The impact caused the air to rush out of her lungs with an embarrassing little scream. She must be dead already, because as she met and clung to him, magnificent wings unfurled behind him then enveloped her in darkness. She was still falling, no, not falling. Diving maybe. For the longest time, waiting for the impact. She felt the warmth of his chest against her cheek and the steady beat of his strong heart. Her mind must have conjured this fantasy to help her cope with the inevitable.

And then it was bright daylight again as his wings unfurled again and began to fly upward. She found herself gazing up at him.

"Hey Elyse," he smiled slightly, softening the intensity of his gaze.

"H...Hey," she stammered back, not able to find the words. "I don't...?"

His smile widened briefly before fleeing from his face, leaving only the intenseness. "Soon, I can explain, just have to get us down this mountain first. I'm Adrian."

Elyse nodded, as the wind whistled in her ears and she became aware of the thinness of the freezing cold air. She was only now realising how high they were. The snowy peak of Far Mountain loomed just ahead of them. The magnificence of it made her gasp, or maybe it was the altitude because she was starting to feel a little dizzy. The microscopic turquoise and blue world below was disappearing in a hazy mauve fog and somewhere far below she saw the ominously dark, wedged shape of the flyer. It could not ascend to this height despite its modern enhancements.

Then they were up and over the peak and gliding gently downwards in ever increasing arcs towards the ground. Elyse looked up at Adrian's wings, the long flight feathers lifting and settling in the strong updrafts while the shorter ones fluttered madly. Then she drank in his closeness and the chiselled perfection of his features. What was this magical creature, half man, half eagle? She should have been scared or shocked or something but all she felt was exhilaration and excitement.

Adrian became aware of her gaze and looked back at her, trying not to show how incredibly happy he was not to have to hide who and what he was. And how good it felt to hold her slight, delicate form so close to him. A subtle strength flowed through her. He hadn't quite believed it when she had dived headfirst from the mountain. The bravery that took for someone who couldn't fly astounded him.

Even though he knew that the Sky-flyer had no hope of following his swift manoeuvres, Adrian flew further away from the town than was necessary, just to prolong the pure joy of holding her in his arms. He couldn't risk returning to the meeting place until the pilot had given up the search and he knew just the place to hide her until it was safe to return.

A grassy glade, hidden by tall trees that shivered silvery blue in the sunshine, complete with pond and a cabin he and his father had built when he was a child and his brothers were still infants. Even though it was largely unused, his dad still kept it clean and waterproof.

Adrian smiled as Elyse sighed with appreciation upon walking in. Cosy, colourful and comfortable. A fire place waited to be brought to life under a rough-hewn mantle draped with greenery and berries. Gratefully she slipped the backpack from her shoulders and sank into the soft looking couch. Adrian sat down beside her. So close that she could almost feel his warmth. She leaned closer, took his large hand in both her smaller ones and held it captured in a silent thank you, before reluctantly letting him go. She was in danger of forgetting her mission if she stayed in such close proximity, but for the life of her, she couldn't summon the strength to increase the distance between them.

Elyse was so used to keeping the details of her discovery secret, but if this man, or angel or whatever he was had wanted to harm her or stop her finding the plant, then he had ample opportunity. She was uncomfortably aware that he had been on the fringes of her life for a few days now, maybe longer, following her. Now he had placed himself between her and danger. He had proved himself worthy of her trust.

"Thank you so much for saving me, and saving my samples," Elyse smiled at him.

"Your work is so important," he replied, "for the whole world. More, than even you realise. It has been my honour to be your Guardian."

"What do you mean, 'even more than I realise?'" she questioned.

"I can't tell you that yet. It is not my information to give, but I will take you to those who can. We have to rest now. It is too cold to fly now. We will leave at first light."

"Will your wings ice up?" she laughed.

"As a matter of fact, no, but your hair might," he replied with a grin.

"How do they fit under your shirt anyway?" she asked without thinking. The thought of touching the warm skin of his back crept into her mind and she shook her hair across her face to hide her flushed cheeks.

Adrian leant closer and gently pushed her hair back over her ears. The movement sent tingles across her skin. He leaned in closer until their breaths mingled. Elyse began to feel so very strange. Her vision dimmed as the room was bathed in a soft violet glow.

"Sorry," he whispered, clearing his throat, and pulled away. This would not do. He had no right to distract her from her work. The future of every creature on this planet depended on it.

And his future included a lifetime of solitude and darkness.

Adrian forced himself stand up and walk away to set a crackling fire and prepare supper, but he needn't have worried because Elyse got up too and followed him into the kitchen, as if she too couldn't bear to be apart from him. They worked together in harmony making a simple meal and when it was done, washing and drying the dishes as if they had done this for a lifetime. How was such synchronicity even possible?

He wondered if she felt it too, but resisted the urge to glance at her. What was he even doing? They had only just met. Yesterday. And there may not even be a tomorrow for them. Adrian decided to stop thinking about the future and just live in the moment.

Evening turned into a velvet night that peered into the windows. It reminded Adrian that there would be an early start in the morning for them both. No matter how much he wished for it, this moment could not last forever.

The cottage had only two rooms. A small bathroom where Elyse was able to freshen up and prepare for bed, and the living area with sleeping benches on either side of the log fire. Elyse chose the one on the right and settled in for some insomnia after the terror and excitement of the day, but found herself drifting off in seconds, listening to the fire in the hearth and the wind outside in the trees.

CHAPTER 11

True to his word, Adrian woke Elyse at first light and smiled at her sleepy clumsiness and dishevelment. Her usual grace had given way to an endearing unsteadiness as she headed for the bathroom. Before long she emerged, more like herself but also more self-conscious than she had been last night. The events of that long and wonderous day had weakened her usual introverted reserve and freed her personality.

Now she felt strange at the familiar and comfortable way they had spent the evening. Adrian felt it too. He had never known a person like Elyse. Multifaceted like a precious gem. Everything he learned about her just made him more enchanted. He looked away. He couldn't pursue this. New Worlders didn't belong here. His people and hers did not interact on many levels. Only the most fleeting and casual contact. That is how his people stayed safe. He had no right to become so close to this girl, for her safety and that of his people. She would return to her own life and he would continue his dark role of Guardian.

"We will have to fly out before daybreak," he said, more abruptly than he intended. Elyse made a slight movement back from him and then nodded seriously.

She packed her things quickly in the dawn dimness before venturing outside with Adrian. Tiny birds sat invisibly on their perches and predicted morning would come. It was a beautiful and complex symphony of hope. The air was crisp and cold. Waiting for the sun's warmth.

Elyse turned to Adrian and could not stop herself drawing in a small breath at his chiselled beauty in the dim light. He had forgotten his resolve and smiled. Her embarrassment at being a clumsy morning mess dissolved into happiness at his closeness. And soon they would soon be closer still. Flying was definitely a contact mode of transport. She hoped, selfishly, that he did not fly like this with anyone else.

As if sensing her thoughts, he grinned, "I'm not used to flying tandem. You'll have to bear with me while I work out the aerodynamics."

"That would be my pleasure," she grinned back and adjusted her backpack before moving into the shelter of his arms. Pressing her cheek into his chest, and wrapping her arms around his waist, she sighed with exhilaration as her feet left the ground. She vaguely thought that she hadn't even asked him where they were going.

They flew towards the sunrise, up and around the mountains resplendent with glittering snowy summits and swooped through the valleys. No Sky-flyers marred the view today. The world below was like a miniature paradise. Elyse suspected they were going the long way around, which still wasn't long enough for her. All too soon, it was over and Adrian deposited her gently on the ground.

She recognised the quaint cobbled streets of Far Mountain town. He had brought her back to the inn. Slivers of sunshine sparkled everywhere.

"There are some people I'd like to introduce you to later today," he said. "I will meet you in the coffee shop after you've rested."

Elyse nodded, already missing him. He stood quietly, waiting for her to enter safely but hoping she would turn around and run into his arms instead. He had to settle for Elyse giving him quick glance over her shoulder as the door closed behind her.

CHAPTER 12

He wasn't sure how his kinfolk would react to this outsider who had climbed their sacred mountain and plundered one of their most precious treasures. That she had discovered its efficacy independently was difficult to comprehend. Her restraint in taking but the smallest specimens and her reticence in publishing her findings would most definitely stand in her favour. As would the gentleness and sweetness of her nature. But the heroism she had shown on Far Mountain, facing a formidable enemy, and choosing to leap to her death, rather than letting the Saurians take her research had shown a courage and commitment that they could not easily dismiss.

He had secretly been appalled at the council's decision not to help Harbour City and New Homeland with the plague, simply to keep their secrets and hide safely in the shadow of Far Mountain. The invasion of the Saurians would be catastrophic on the weakened humans.

That is why he volunteered so quickly to leave all that he knew and loved, to forgo safety, for the dark and violent life of a Guardian and protect the innocent in a far-off land. His first days away from home had been cold and lonely until his brothers had joined him. The city was grey and hard as were the people. Scarred and frightened, they had withdrawn into themselves and moved with a hunched and defensive posture. The parasites had not only taken over their bodies, but had deformed their personalities and locked away the friendliness and joy they must have once had.

Which is why he had first noticed her. Like a shot of colour in the grey world. Hope in the midst of despair. Beauty surrounded by ugliness but untouched by it.

He had begun looking for her at the train station, had noticed how she rubbed her arm waiting for decontamination. He had moved in close enough to observe, but far enough to stay hidden. He had seen the barely visible scarring on her arm, even as she pulled down her sleeve to hide it. He had known then, that she was special. She had survived the microscopic invasion of her body with barely a scar. How had she managed to not only fight off the parasites, but to do it alone. That puzzled him. Her name was not on the register of the infected.

That is when he stopped merely looking for her and started serious surveillance. From her tiny apartment early each morning to the laboratory down town and home again late in the day, she rarely changed her routine. She seemed driven. Took no days off.

He broke into the laboratory after closing hours and was astonished to discover her research. It was heading in a completely different direction from most of the other scientists, and yet it was leading directly to the cure. The cure he was forbidden to share on pain of exile. And then he found her secret. Hidden in the storage vault. Crumbling dry remnants of the precious plant that had kept his own people safe through the millennia. Carefully labelled and stored in a vacuum vial, he felt her presence as he touched the things she had touched. Her hands had carefully withdrawn some of this plant and she had cured herself with it which led to her ongoing successful research.

He was secretly proud of her, even as he wondered how the Far Mountain elders would react to the news of an outsider using their medicines. And now, albeit innocently, she had brought the Saurians back to their peaceful land. Even now, they were hovering somewhere in the Sky-flyer, looking for her. After the gathering, he would have some cleaning up to do. Adrian smiled grimly. Perhaps his brothers Gabe and Cam could join the party.

At least the Saurians would not have been able to signal their Harbour City brethren from Far Mountain. His ancestors, prior to abandoning their life of technology, had erected a selective communication shield over the planet. Invisible, undetectable and effective, it was another layer of safety for their descendants.

CHAPTER 13

Elyse closed the door behind her and leaned on its solid wooden surface gratefully. When she closed her eyes, she felt as if she was still flying madly through the air. Her stomach still doing somersaults with delayed reaction. Nevertheless, it was time to wash and only then could she rest.

Feeling fresh and clean, she sank onto the pillowy bed to sort through her backpack. As she tilted it, the clasp she had dug out of the mountainside fell into her lap. It was beautiful, even caked with pale dirt. When she had washed and polished it, she pulled out her lens and the details were finally revealed.

A perfect replica of her plant, frosted with purple and green jewels grew intertwined with a tiny but glorious grasshopper. It really wasn't a grasshopper, was it? More like a miniature winged deer. What was the significance of the little creature? Was this the missing variable? It made perfect sense. The unidentified organic residue on the original dehydrated specimen in her lab, this could be it. Grasshopper saliva. She couldn't stifle a giggle. The fate of the world may depend on the oral secretions of a sweet but weird little grasshopper deer. It could be the enzymatic action on the plant cells, or remnants of the creature's microbiome. It could also be a more complex interaction, perhaps of antibodies. She had to look through alpine biology records to see if this species had been catalogued. Not many New Homelanders had ventured into these mountains. She was aware of several botanists who had made the trek up Far Mountain and brought back plant specimens, but knew of no etymologists who had studied the insects here and it was definitely not her area of expertise.

This clasp needed to be protected, just as the plant. Not something she could just carry around in a back pack. Where could she put it that would keep it safe, and close? Looking down, Elyse saw the cloth sash that cinched her gown. She would hide it in plain sight. Threading the sash through the back of the clasp she tied it carefully around her waist. Perfect. No one would give it a second glance.

Taking great care, Elyse took the container with the plant leaves, embedded in growing gel medium from the padded pocket at the front of her backpack. Something amazing had happened since yesterday. The plants had grown. Two more iridescent, furry leaves had joined to the base of each of the original leaf stems and a mass of tiny rootlets had begun to fill replace the gel. It looked happy to be in a nice warm spot. The thought made Elyse smile as she slid them gently back into the pocket for safekeeping.

Time to have a coffee and some Sweetberry pie!

He was waiting for her in his usual spot, back against the wall. No cap today, his black hair shone like a bird's wing in the sunlight streaming into the coffee shop. His eyes never left her face as she crossed the space between them. Elyse slid into the chair across from him. The handsome older man she had met, was it only yesterday, came up to their table, smiling in welcome.

"Elyse, meet my father, Constantine... Dad, this is Elyse, the friend I was telling you about."

Constantine's smile widened. "Ahh, Elyse, good to put a face to the name. I've been looking forward to meeting Adrian's city friend. How do you like our little town?"

"It is just marvellous!" she laughed. "More beautiful than the photos I've seen, and your son has given me a wonderful tour of some really impressive landscapes."

"Ha! I bet he has!" Laughing, Constantine took their orders.

All too soon it was time to head to the meeting hall. Elyse felt nervous. She had spent a lifetime pretty much isolated apart from brief exchanges with fellow scientists, communicating strictly about their work. Even talking to two people at a time was difficult. How was she going to manage a whole gathering?

Adrian must have sensed her reticence, because as they made their way up through the cobbled streets, he intertwined his fingers with hers gently. His strength flowed into her with quiet calm and they walked in step as though they had done this their entire lives. What was it about this man that made her feel so capable, so protected? Might be the wings...or maybe the swooping...definitely the swooping...and the wings. And the steady beat of his heart when he held her close.

She needn't have worried, Adrian's people welcomed her with warm friendliness. From colourfully dressed children to silver haired elders they greeted her as if she was an old and dear friend. She found herself swept away from Adrian towards the front of the hall. As she turned to glance back at him, his eyes locked onto hers, even as two other young men who could have been his brothers, from their easy strength and good looks, joined him and punched him playfully. Elyse let herself enjoy the moment. This must be what having family and friends would be like. Felt wonderful.

The meeting began soon after her arrival. Adrian introduced Elyse to everyone as a New Worlder who had defeated the scourge even as the parasites had threatened to engulf her, by turning to the ancient wisdom of their people. He recounted her sensitivity with the information she had gathered and the gentle way she had treated the alpine plants. The hushed room erupted into whistles of admiration as he recounted her dive from the mountain to protect their secrets.

Elyse found herself flushing, not used to being the centre of attention. It was her turn.

"It was serendipity," she explained humbly. "I am so lucky to be a project scientist, working as part of the world-wide team dedicated to finding a cure. Even more lucky to have an ancient repository of botanical specimens to study. The plants that grow near the summit of Far Mountain have always fascinated me. Eking out a life in one of the most inhospitable places on the planet. Barely enough rocky soil to sink their roots into. Soaring temperatures by day with intense solar radiation, freezing each night. Their cells become solid, lifeless and bristling with icicles but with the morning sun they defrost and live again.

I thought that was in fact this freeze and thaw that contained the answer I was looking for. But I now believe it wasn't the plants alone which, after all, have a relatively simple structure, but in a small and seemingly insignificant insect that shares not only the habitat of the plant I have been studying, but its amazing biological cycle of life. This tiny, I am not sure what it is, but I will call it a grasshopper, feeds on the plant each day, then finds shelter in the nearest tiny crag and freezes next to it at night.

Freezes completely. No heartbeat, no respiration, no brain activity. It is for all intents and purposes completely dead. And in the morning, as the sun's rays find the grasshopper's shiny wings, it comes to life again. And with it comes an unbelievable regeneration of tissues. Wounds heal, nerves regrow, infections are defeated.

It is the interaction of animal and plant that create the scientific magic which prevented the spread of the parasites in my arm." As Elyse lifted her arm, her sleeve fell away, showing the shadow but not the scar that should be there. "And there is something else, the parasites are working as an organised community. They seem to be intelligent creatures with an agenda. I saw them building structures and communicating with each other."

Everyone murmured at this point and she paused to let her words permeate the corners of the hall.

"I found an organic residue on the dried specimen I used which I couldn't identify, but I believe it is from the little grasshopper and could be salvation for the entire planet. This information must remain a secret. If the corporations find out, they will plunder your land in their haste and greed. I must take this knowledge home with me and synthesise a treatment which will help my people without harming yours."

Applause erupted and a sense of relief was felt by all, she was sure. They were too kind and generous not to feel guilty about keeping their age-old secret while the world suffered. This plan was the best of both worlds.

At the back of the hall, flanked by his friends, Adrian felt a rush of pride at Elyse's elegant solution. And more than a little regret that the Guardians had not even tried to find an alternative to simply protecting their own at the cost of innocents everywhere.

After the meeting, supper was served in the courtyard. Platters of fresh fruits and vegetables, sprinkled with flowers, small cakes courtesy of Constantine's bakery. And blue green herbal drinks which Elyse would find out had a bit of a secret zing. She found herself refreshed and recharged by the freshness of the food she ate. There was no greyish vitamised New Homeland slosh here. Her brain continued to steam ahead. Nutrition had to be another part of the equation. How could anyone be truly healthy while eating things that were created rather than grown?

Small candles had been strung in the branches overhanging the courtyard. Lacy metal tables adorned the pavement with even more candles. A soft glow enveloped the sheltered garden. Music played somewhere in the background. One of Far Mountain's less-known melodies, but equally sad and beautiful, like Funeral for the World.

In the back of her mind, the worry about the Sky-flyer nagged, and the need to return to her lab to continue her work, but she pushed her thoughts aside to enjoy the peaceful harmony of this place and these people at least for a while longer. The women had drawn her into their circle and were including her in their conversations. As she laughed and answered their questions of life in Harbour City, she wished she was one of them fully and utterly. Even now, she felt closer to them than she had felt with anyone in her home town.

Her eyes were involuntarily drawn to the far corner of the courtyard where Adrian was in deep conversation with the two young men she had seen before. They seemed to be in a heated discussion. As if one they turned and looked at her, as if deciding something, then separated. The others disappeared into the dimness of the building and Adrian strode towards Elyse with a look of determination on his face.

"Come with me," he asked urgently as he neared her, "before they change their minds."

"Where?" she asked. He was already moving away and she had to rush a little to put down her plate and race after him. What was going on?

Adrian led her into a smaller room adorned with tapestries of battle scenes that looked very old. A large oval table in the centre of the space was surrounded by high backed chairs adorned with carvings of alpine plants and flowers. Only two chairs remained vacant, the rest were occupied by elders and Adrian's friends and father. No one spoke. The contrast between this meeting and the previous was not lost on Elyse and she found herself nervous and worried once again. Adrian pulled out a chair for her, taking care not to touch her in any way and sat down beside her. He seemed uneasy as well.

One of the elders cleared his throat and straightened in his chair. From her days as a musician, she knew the signs of an imminent solo performance. She wasn't mistaken. Seconds later, the chair scraped back and he stood up.

"Welcome child," he spoke in a soft but commanding voice. "I am Marcus. Welcome to our circle. We have debated the merits of sharing our knowledge with an outsider, but your courageous actions both in developing a cure independently and being willing to protect our mountain's secrets with your life, has made our choice unanimous.

Child, you have stumbled upon an invasion a thousand eons in the making. The plague is just the beginning. A way to weaken the population not only physically but sociologically and emotionally. Breaking the bonds of friendship and the closeness of family. Minimising freedom of thought, expression and action. We have been fortunate to keep Far Mountain isolated but safety is only an illusion. Our immunity is not certain even though we are more resistant than the New Homelanders.

The next wave will not involve parasitic attackers but lizard like Saurians from beyond the stars with superior physical capabilities and generations of preparation. The world will not stand a chance. No person or animal can withstand their attack. Not even the Liroons, the grasshoppers that you mentioned. There will be no one at the funeral to come."

Waves of dread trickled down Elyse's spine at his words. Maybe it would have been better if she had never stumbled onto this knowledge. She could have lived simply and contentedly in her lab until it happened, thinking the infection was the only challenge. No. It was never her way to sit back and accept the inevitable. Her need to change destiny was the reason she was sitting in this room while the enormity of the task ahead was laid out before her.

"What can I do?" she asked with her natural directness.

Everyone smiled as one and several people clapped appreciatively.

A female elder replied, "Your actions have already set your people on the road to resurgence. You must continue your work. Complete your serum. You must share your knowledge with your people. You must make them well and prepare them for the battle ahead. And you must do it quickly."

Elyse shook her head. "My work yes. But I am no leader, I am invisible. I cannot make anyone listen to me."

The elder smiled wisely. "They will hear the happy voices of their loved ones as they heal and they will listen. You won't be alone. We will send our best Guardians. You have already met Adrian." She waved across the table, "and these young men are his brothers Gabe and Cam. There are other teams spread across the New World."

The three men nodded solemnly well aware of the enormity of their mission. A few against countless. The Saurians they had erased so far had been only the few scattered sentinels. The vast majority lived underground. Waiting.

It was time to go. Elyse's respite from the greyness of Harbour City was at an end. A dull ache tightened in her chest. Sadness and fear supplanted the exhilaration and liberty of the last few days.

But she wouldn't be going alone. The best part of Far Mountain was accompanying her home. She glanced at his profile and breathed more easily. With him in her life, no matter what happened next, she was happier than she had ever been.

CHAPTER 14

Kirsten.

When the pen had started shaking so badly in her hand that she couldn't even read her own writing, Kirsten had turned to a mechanical writer. If she rested her thin scarred forearms into the curved splints attached to her desk, her withered fingers were in the right position to touch the keys but it took every ounce of strength she had to press them with enough force to make a dent in the parchment.

The manuscript was growing painfully slowly. The urgency of her research coupled with the ever-decreasing abilities of her body, filled Kirsten's busy mind with frustration. So many puzzle pieces to fit together, so many that didn't belong. Even before the disease had progressed, her fingers had not been able to keep up with her brain. Even when she slept, her mind continued to race. She had nightmarish visions of grey lizards crawling inside her body and woke to silent screaming.

Something was very wrong. Over and above the obvious pandemic that was sweeping the world and leaving pain and death in its wake. There was something more. Something was coming. Something bad. Harbour City was doomed despite the major inroads the medical fraternity was making in controlling the spread of the infection. If only it was a simple infection.

Encountering a clay frieze during a chance visit to the museum of ancient artifacts had changed her perception of everything she had ever known. It depicted writhing figures, obviously in agony by the looks on their faces being attacked by creatures that looked like two legged lizards. The same lizards she had seen in her dreams.

Some were life sized, attacking humans with their wicked teeth and some were like ants fighting small, beautiful creatures with antlers. If she hadn't had such excellent vision, Kirsten would have thought they were barely scratch marks in the clay. Above the battle flew the figure of what looked to be a winged man with a serene, handsome face and beautifully defined muscles.

Were these unknown creatures real? Had they been inhabitants of this world or had they arrived from another? Scarce historical data had hindered her early research and she had almost given up.

And then, late one day when she was snuggling into her cloak while being driven back from the water unit where she had received stretching in the warm therapy pool, she saw him. Her driver had taken a short cut through the dimly lit underground. The road filled her with fear even though she knew the vehicle was impenetrable. Underground was teeming with the infected. They were huddling by low fires or lying under makeshift shelters. No one should have to live like this.

The vehicle had slowed to a crawl, backed up behind others. Kirsten, enjoying the movement her stretching therapy had given her, leaned onto the window to peer out at them. What she saw shook her to the core. A lizard creature, almost exactly like the one she had seen on the frieze, was standing over a person lying by one of the fires.

Dread filled Kirsten as she realised the sort of terror she was about to witness. As the lizard lifted one thin arm over his head, ready to strike, the most amazing thing she had ever seen happened.

Her vision dimmed, as though a violet fog surrounded her vehicle. From the darkness, a winged man dove, swift and deadly, straight into the lizard who vanished in an explosion of grey liquid. The man landed beside the person by the fire and his wings folded, disappearing under his swirling cape. Illuminated by firelight, even from a distance, his golden perfection was visible. Kirsten couldn't see his face, only the darkness of his hair, but she could imagine it.

And then, as if feeling the intensity of her gaze, he turned and looked right at her. Her breath caught in her chest as their eyes met. Not recognition, but some feeling beyond anything Kirsten had ever experienced rushed through her brain and into her body. She wished she could freeze time and live single moment forever, but her vehicle was moving slowly out of the line of sight.

From that night, Kirsten redoubled her efforts to track down historical data of winged men and reptiles. She hired a confidential fetcher to bring tomes from the historical record repository and had pored through them one by one until she found what she was looking for in the most unlikely place. In an illustrated children's story book. FAIRY TALES OF FAR MOUNTAIN.

Gently opening the book and turning the slightly yellowed parchment pages, Kirsten read.

Once upon a time, a tiny village sheltered under a tall mountain which protected it. One day, a flying ship from the planet Saurian, landed in the middle of the village. Monsters, large and small attacked the villagers or made them sick.

The mountain opened, and in a beam of purple light, released its Guardians, who drove the monsters, deep underground. Plants and animals joined with all the villagers and Guardians for a celebration. Everyone rejoiced.

Kirsten smiled. Her hero was a guardian from a fairy tale. That probably made her a damsel in distress. She was beyond wishing for someone to save her. The most she could wish for was to die before she ran out of the means to stay in her safe, warm apartment. The means to have masked and gowned support staff tend to her physical needs until she had finished her research and brought her people one step closer to defeating the plague.

The more she thought about her Guardian, the more he appeared in her dreams. Surrounded by shimmering violet light, he reached for her until her longing would wake her up to the grimness of reality. Her dreams became more intense, more passionate and the contrast between them and the bleakness of her life intensified too.

The only reason she woke up each morning was to continue her research because she knew now that he wasn't just a dream. And just maybe he could be the answer the entire world was searching for.

It was a race against time and time won, just as she found the third piece of the puzzle, an ancient illustrated text, an alchemy book of spells. Spells ranging from hair growth potions to true love tisanes. But the one that interested her most was the Far Mountain tremor cure. The ingredients were largely indecipherable on the yellowed parchment but it was the illustration which caught her attention. It showed a beautiful insect, something that looked like a cross between a grasshopper and an antelope, probably long extinct. The page was adorned with finely drawn leaves and flowers and a perfect image of Far Mountain as the backdrop. This must be it. The legendary tea that the Guardians had fed the villagers in her fairy tale. She needed to find someone to decipher the recipe while she could still move. Someone who could continue and complete her work.

The tremors were increasing. Her head had started flopping down at odd moments while she stayed fully conscious but unable to move a muscle. She couldn't even blink for a while before recovering. It was as if her lifeforce was flickering faintly in the darkness then flaring and would soon wink out.

That is how they found her as she half sat, half lay over her writer. The keys making little square indents in her slack cheek. Kirsten's one unobstructed eye followed them as they invaded her sanctuary and wreaked havoc on her apartment. Cushions flew from the armchairs, books and a vase of flowers crashed onto the floor, lamps sailed across the room and smashed against the walls. Furniture was upended and torn apart. It was a violent attack with no discernible purpose or meaning.

Maybe they were vandals who hated furniture. Sooner or later, they would get to her because at the moment she was about as useful as a piece furniture.

One of the attackers sensed Kirsten's gaze and leant down over her. It was a female. Tall and impossibly thin. Hair gelled into wicked spikes and makeup designed to shock with no eyebrows, overdone black smoky eyes and grey lipstick. As the woman bent closer, Kirsten realized it wasn't lipstick. It was skin. She looked into the woman's eyes and was shocked to see vertical ellipses for pupils with pale yellow irises as a second eyelid slid across them. An unpleasantly strong perfume emanated from the creature which almost hid the smell of dankness. A blueish forked tongue flicked swiftly in and out of the lizard woman's grey mouth.

Kirsten stared back at her, unable to look away. Apparently not satisfied that her victim was alive, the creature pressed her fingertips to Kirsten's neck, feeling for the feeble heartbeat that was counting down the remaining days of her life. The fingers were icy cold. Combined with the overpowering perfume, the chill made Kirsten sneeze hard.

The strength returned to her upper body and Kirsten was able to sit upright. A wave of dizziness from the sudden change of position and a rushing sound in her ears was almost overwhelming and Kirsten shut her eyes tightly until the tide had receded. When she opened them again another reptilian stood over her. With the same yellow eyes and theatrical makeup, he looked like the woman's twin.

"You've had your fun, now please leave!" Kirsten was dismayed. Her sarcastic command sounded tremulous and high pitched. Definitely not the voice of someone who expected to be obeyed. She was right, they turned away and ignored her completely. With brisk efficiency, the male scooped up her papers, picked up her writer and stowed everything in a satchel. A chilling realization came over her. These were no random vandals; they were here to steal her research.

Kirsten opened her mouth to protest, but closed it again, deciding it would be an exercise in futility. Their cold, blank stares brooked no opposition. The female leading the pack sneered at her as the others rustled through her things.

"Mara!" one of the others called across the room. "Ready!"

Unfortunately, they were not stopping at her research. The woman called Mara pulled out a syringe and moved towards Kirsten who tried to wave her away with a pathetic and futile gesture of her trembling hand. It was no use. She felt a sting in her neck. For a second the soft wings of her Guardian enveloped her and he touched her lips with his as she arched backwards into oblivion.

CHAPTER 15

Coming home that evening was surreal. After experiencing the freshness and colour of Far Mountain, the glass towers and greyness of Harbour City seemed strange and foreign. Elyse felt a familiar depression try to settle over her but it vanished into happiness as she turned her head. Adrian grinned as though reading her thoughts and just barely resisted the urge to thread his fingers through hers. His brothers were far enough away and would not see the gesture, but he didn't want to risk the complication of them knowing just how close he had become with this New Homelander, even though he knew they would never betray his trust. They were closer than most brothers while growing up. The time they had spent separated, fighting the Saurians had only strengthened their unspoken bond.

They would separate again now, to cover more ground and erase more of the enemy. Adrian would stay with Elyse and help her complete the serum. Then together they would overcome the invaders once and for all.

She felt so tired as they neared her building. It had been a long day and she was looking forward to sinking into her own bed and just sleeping until the sun came up over the skyscrapers.

The door to her apartment was hanging crookedly on one hinge. It looked weirdly forlorn, as if it had tried to bar an intruder and failed miserably. Adrian gently placed his arm in front of her, carefully opened the door and walked into the apartment.

They had obviously been there days before her. Searching. Total devastation surrounded her. Every chair had been upended and slashed. Drawers were opened and contents strewn across the apartment. Her favourite couch was just a piece of rubble. Even the kitchen had not been spared. What had they hoped to find in the dish drainer or the flour jar?

Her once lush boxed houseplants and window herbs were nothing but shrivelled victims of the violence. She had been emotionally attached to each and every one of them. Elyse sank down next to her most beloved tree and touched its crinkly leaves gently. She wished she had been here to stop them, but then, maybe she would also be lying here, slowly disintegrating into the carpet. Even worse, they could have taken the research papers and specimens from her pack and the Saurian victory would have been assured.

Adrian touched her shoulder quietly and she looked up into his concerned eyes. "We should go," he whispered quietly. "There is nothing we can do here now."

Elyse nodded and allowed him to help her up. Turning her back on the domestic mayhem was easier than having to deal with it tonight. They had to go to her lab. She had to start work on the serum. There was no time to sleep now.

More devastation greeted them there.

A police band stretched across the doorway which Adrian detached from one end, allowing them access. Here, the searchers had been even more thorough. Petri dishes and test tubes lay smashed everywhere. Growing medium had dried to powder on the floor.

Elyse tiptoed over the crushed glass which tinkled under her feet and made her way to the plant repository. She gasped when she saw the utter chaos. It made her faintly queasy to see so many irreplaceable specimens simply ground into the floor. If she hadn't already taken and used the alpine plant to cure herself months ago, it too may have been laying crushed and useless here. All hope would have been lost. Her fingers tightened protectively over the tiny plants that lay hidden safely in her backpack.

She had work to do. She would not let this destructive enemy win. Forcing the despair from her heart, she summoned optimism and determination.

Turning to Adrian who stood uncharacteristically slumped behind her she smiled and tapped him playfully on the shoulder.

"Chin up!" she advised, "food first, then we slay these dragons with science! I need to buy a growing box and some gel for my specimens."

Adrian straightened, surprised at her reaction and smiled back, somewhat uncertainly to start with, but then with purpose as her optimism caught hold. "Sounds like a plan. Let's get some supplies, and food. We can use my living quarters as your makeshift lab, there is plenty of room."

It was an understatement, as he lived in a warehouse that had been converted into a loft with castle-like proportions right on the harbour. It had been abandoned by the wealthy owner when the harbour revitalization project failed after the plague took hold and was a perfect refuge for Adrian and the other Dark Guardians. The signs of new money remained in the sleek designer furnishings and artistic statement lights. He kept the place blindingly neat. It was rarely used for anything but sleep after a long day's hunting.

Elyse raised both eyebrows as Adrian ushered her in. His place was absolutely stunning. From the multiple arched windows to the oversized couches to the cathedral like proportions, it was the opposite of her imaginings. She supposed that her first impression of a homeless street musician had set her imagination on his home in Harbour City being somewhat meagre and gloomy, completely unlike this magnificent architectural homage to the ancient ruins beyond the city.

"Wow, you are not kidding, you have so much room. My whole apartment would fit in one corner. And it is just beautiful."

Before she did anything else, Elyse freed the tiny plants from the dark pocket of her backpack. The gel at the base of the tub had been completely replaced by rootlets and the top had been gapped open by leaves pushing their way out. She took the top off completely and the plants unfurled into that perfect rosette shape she had seen on the mountain. They had not wasted any time, growing madly, as if they knew how incredibly important they were.

Setting up the growing boxes next to a window which already sported a few arching boxed trees, Elyse released the plants which continued to expand and grow before her eyes. She hoped against hope that the marauders would never find this place from the destruction they had wreaked on her own houseplants. As she moved away, she gently touched the tips of the leaves, feeling their energy mingle with hers.

Adrian explained that he and his brothers each used the loft when they were in Harbour City, even though they rarely saw one another, as he pulled out plates and cutlery to serve the food they had bought in style. Eating at the table, with candles lit and wine glowing in tall, curved glasses, Elyse was tempted to relax and stay a while longer, but she made herself stand up as soon as she could muster the energy and unpack the laboratory supplies that they had bought.

To create the serum, she first had to isolate the active factor from the alpine plant's leaves, then reproduce it, test it and replicate it. It was no easy task. The first time she had done it was basic and clumsy. She had simply muddled the leaves into a sterile medium, strained the resulting fluid. Simple contact with the fluid had killed the parasites, not only where it had contacted them on the microscope plate, but in her body as well.

They were somehow connected. Perhaps chemically, neurally - an invisible link. It had happened so quickly that she had not been able to test her theory. Interestingly, the effect was not far reaching. It was something small. She needed her microscope.

The first leaf looked even more spectacular under the microscope. Its surface was coated in transparent, rainbow glistening hairs, each of which was tipped with droplets of fluid that shimmered under the light. Tiny holes had been chewed into the leaves' edges, probably by the Liroon. As she held the slide, Elyse turned her microscope to the invisible spectrum and dimmed the overhead lights. What she saw gave her waves upon wave of goosebumps.

Streams of purple light flowed from the tips of the plant's furry, chewed edges, interconnecting and weaving. Enveloping the microscope and invisibly caressing her finger. She gently moved her hand towards the plant and the light strengthened and shimmered. She pulled away and the streams dulled and centralized around the damaged leaf parts.

Light. It wasn't inconceivable that light was the missing factor. The method by which the plant and animal combined to form such a potent remedy, perhaps even cure for the infection or infestation. If she could identify the wavelength, isolate it and then harness it...

Adrian interrupted her study by touching her gently on the shoulder. She looked up to tell him her news but the words never escaped her mouth as she saw his worried frown.

"I've just heard from Gabe. He has been patrolling the north side of the city and has tracked a group of Saurians who seem to have a New Homelander held hostage." Adrian's frown increased. "He plans to neutralize them alone and rescue their prisoner. There are too many of them. Cam and I have to help him but I don't want to leave you here alone."

"I won't open the door to anyone," Elyse tried to make light of the situation as she saw him to the door and locked it behind him. He left a searing silence with his absence. It was ridiculous. She had been alone for most of her life. It had seemed incredibly normal, but now she felt bereft, as if now she was only half of something. How hard had it been to gain independence and strength, how easy to lose it.

A small voice told her that it wasn't a loss of independence that Adrian had brought, but a deep companionship that was as addictive as it was needed by her soul. She smiled at her revelation, feeling better, and turned back to her microscope.

CHAPTER 16

Gabe loved his job. The freedom from the mundane niceties of village life at Far Mountain no matter how sweet the place of his birth was. The challenge of the hunt, being able to rescue people without them even seeing his face. Even the kill. The Saurians were so patently evil and unredeemable. He felt no remorse as their bodies turned into slime and oozed back into the depths where they belonged.

He had no ties to the New Homeland either. Harbour City had become a cold and grey place under the cloud of the plague. It made life so much easier to just fly wherever his wings took him. No one in the city ever looked up. They were so engrossed in their own misery.

His only true friends were his brothers and the other Guardians. They were the only ones who truly understood this dark life. But they were different. Adrian agonised over every target he had taken out. And the older he became, the more torn he was. And Cam was just too cheerful. Everything was mildly amusing to him and Gabe had no idea what was lurking behind his casual smile. Even as boys, they got along as close as brothers could be while being so dissimilar in personality and approach. It didn't matter. They had a job to do. He was happy in his self-enforced isolation. It made him almost invulnerable.

So, when he had locked eyes with the most beautiful but fragile girl he had ever seen in the dimness of the underground tunnels, just as he had completed a kill, his world had rocked. She looked back at him, not with fear or revulsion, but with wonder. And then she was gone. By the time he had regained his senses, her transport had vanished beyond the darkness.

That was the first night he had dreamed. Until then he had slept soundly, undisturbed by his subconscious. But now, his rest was punctuated by the most vivid and passionate visions of the girl he had seen ever so briefly. He would wake frustrated and angry at being torn away from her. He continued his work, but could no longer give it his full attention. He was always searching for her. Every street, every building. Nothing.

He had almost given up.

On his regular patrol, something unusual had happened. A group of Saurians who had been acting uncharacteristically, moving with coordination and a lack of stealth, led by an impossibly tall female, entered an apartment block, only to emerge a short time later carrying their prey.

It was his dream girl. She was even more frail than the last time he had seen her. A long silk night gown could not hide her almost painful slimness. Her skin was parchment dry and almost translucent. Long dark hair tumbled towards the ground. Her neck seemed to lack the strength to hold her head up. And yet she even more beautiful than the last time he saw her. Gabe realized that she wasn't even trying to hold her head up. Her eyes were closed. She was unconscious. He could see her chest moving ever so slightly as she breathed. At least she was alive.

Tendrils of fear wrapped around him. This time, he would not lose her. Fading back into the shadows, he waited patiently until the Saurians had taken her into their transport and powered away before following, high and far enough away not to be detected, while sending Adrian and Cam a message. He could not risk her safety by trying to rescue her on his own, much as his pride wanted him to. This time he needed his Guardian brothers.

By the time the Saurians had reached the ancient castle beyond Harbour City, Adrian and Cam were by his side. Together they watched the group carry the still unconscious woman into the ruins. She looked unharmed from this distance but Gabe's levels of fear for her intensified along with an ever-increasing burn of anger. When they had disappeared from view, he looked back at his brothers.

Cam was smiling a little more grimly than usual, the only clue that he too was angry and Adrian looked impatient and ready for action. It looked as though he wanted this adventure to be over and that he had somewhere better to be. After meeting Elyse, Gabe could understand. He turned back to look at the building.

Light flared and faded through the arched windows in the only remaining tower. They could see outlines slithering in the firelight. It was the Saurians, scurrying around. Two legged lizards. Even from this distance they looked ugly and alien. As the guardians watched, all movement stopped. As one they spun around, looking down at something. Gabe thought he heard a woman's voice, calling out in fear. It was time to go in.

CHAPTER 17

Kirsten felt a complete absence of pain as she started to regain consciousness. It was a wonderful sensation. Her hands felt like bird's wings and her toes moved easily, without restriction. Even her brain felt light, a balloon filled with air that floated above the ground. She heard a rustling of wind in leaves, growing increasing loud and irritating. With it the stiffness and pain returned. All the months of growing accustomed to agony had vanished leaving her defenceless against its onslaught. Lying motionless on a cold stone plinth that dug into all the bony points in her body and chilled her to the core.

She wanted to die.

The noises in her head became more distinct, not windblown leaves but voices whispering around her. Harsh, whistling whispers that sounded unlike anything she had heard before. And with the sounds came a nasty, dank smell. Kirsten's nose wrinkled in distaste.

Memory slowly returned. Creatures had invaded her room. They had injected her with something. Drugged her. Maybe they were still there in her room. She briefly considered pretending to sleep but the temptation to see was overwhelming and she opened her eyes. Flickering candlelight glanced off an ancient stone wall, punctuated by arched windows which had long ago lost their glass. Not at home then. Very slowly and painfully she turned her head, and screamed, as a grey skinned, lizard like man moved towards her, sharp teeth bared, vertical pupils narrowing as he realized she was awake.

Her scream barely registered. Damn this weakness. It was enough, however, to alert the female who moved to tower over Kirsten menacingly.

A feeble adrenalin rush flowed through Kirsten's useless body. She no longer wanted to die. She wanted fight, to run, to anything but lie here vulnerable, in her night clothes like a half-dressed mannequin waiting to be dismantled.

The lizards moved closer, their secondary eyelids sliding open and shut. Tongues flicked in her direction. Her chest tightened and tightened until no air could enter, she felt the familiar waves of darkness descending and welcomed impending oblivion.

Then suddenly, dimness exploded into purple light. Startled, Kirsten turned her head. He was here! Her guardian angel, her dream man, strong and gloriously angry. He barely glanced at her before locking eyes with the tall female and flying straight at her, knocking her across the room to hit the far wall with a thud. She skidded to a halt with her elongated limbs articulated into odd angles and scurried on all fours from the room. The others snarled and charged towards him only to be showered in glass shards as two more angels broke through the windows.

Kirsten's eyes watered as she tried to keep up with the fighting around her. Lizard men were thrown like lumps of slime against the stone walls of the abandoned castle and twisted into bizarre shapes. They roared in pain and fell, beyond her line of sight. She felt the air rushing through her lungs as hope returned and she closed her eyes tightly to stem the flow of relieved tears.

And then it was over. No movement, no sound. Even the unpleasant smell had gone.

"Is she alive?" she heard a voice above her ask. She felt a warmth on her face.

Kirsten opened her eyes to see him leaning over her. So close that if she could have lifted her head, she could have kissed him. As if reading her mind, he smiled slowly and bent in closer until his lips met hers and the purple light around her changed to gold. His kiss deepened as he slid his arm under her shoulders and lifted her firmly to his chest. Her dreams were such a pale imitation of the pleasure she felt as his lips moved across hers.

A chuckle from one of the other angels brought them back to reality and he reluctantly released her. Kirsten felt bereft and frustrated and strangely stronger than she had been in a long time. He looked at her with a blazing intensity of passion that told her, beyond words, that he felt the same way.

Clearing his throat, he finally replied, "Yup," as if he couldn't trust himself to say any more. He knew his brothers wouldn't judge him. They were the most supportive family he could ever wish for, but there was another problem ahead of him. There would be hell to pay when the Elders found out that he had kissed a New World woman...and that he intended to kiss her again and often and forever.

"Do you know each other?" the other angel probed, still grinning.

"Not exactly." Not taking his eyes off Kirsten, he addressed her. "I'm Gabe, this smirker is Cam and the serious one is Adrian."

Cam laughed, "I can't help it if life is just so much fun, not to mention how hilarious this situation is. You've obviously captured my cold brother's heart!"

"Kirsten..." she replied flushing, and pulling away "Thank you so much for the rescue. I think they were about to kill me. Don't know why. But...but I'm infected! You shouldn't be so close." Kirsten was proud of how steady her voice was. If only she could move and regain some of her pride. Being a damsel was so not her usual style.

Gabe shook his head, "Don't worry. Those parasites can't hurt us. We're from Far Mountain." He spoke as if that explained everything. Kirsten nodded. She didn't have to ask him what he meant.

"We should go," the serious one said, "Before that lizard comes back with some more friends. Let us meet at my place. Elyse will be glad of some female company."

"I...I can't move," Kirsten said sadly. "It's nothing new, haven't been able to for months now."

"Not a problem," Gabe replied lightly. He wrapped his cloak around her thin frame and scooped her up into his arms. Kirsten's head arched back involuntarily, exposing her delicate throat. It was difficult to resist the temptation to kiss her again, so he adjusted his hold to cradle her head close to his chest instead, not wanting to take advantage of her when she was so defenceless. "Gives me a chance to get close to you again," he murmured against her hair.

For the longest second, nothing else mattered. Not her terminal immobility, not the fact that alien creatures were trying to kill her, not even that they had an audience. Being held by Gabe was as natural as breathing. How a man as beautiful as he was could feel the same way about her was a complete mystery, and, at this moment mattered even less.

She knew he had wings. She had seen them from her transport. But now, as he unfurled the long feathers and caressed her arm with them, she gasped with wonder at his magnificence. The wonder wasn't over yet. As Gabe stepped onto the ledge of the battlements, she felt the wind. His wings spread wide and they lifted into the air together. Kirsten sighed. She could no longer walk but she was made for flying.

CHAPTER 18

All too soon it was over and they had landed on another ledge. Giant arched windows opened and Gabe carried her across the threshold into an enormous room.

Adrian was already there. He and the gracefully shy young woman beside him turned towards them and both smiled in welcome. The frown had disappeared from Adrian's face and he looked somehow younger without it.

"Come in," he invited. "Kirsten, this is Elyse," he added as he smiled down at her.

"So good to have another girl around," Elyse whispered, "come and relax on the couch or would you rather me help you freshen up? And maybe some warm clothes."

Kirsten was grateful for her thoughtfulness. Elyse seemed to have observed and understood Kirsten's weakness and bypassed the awkwardness with friendly warmth. "I wouldn't mind freshening up," Kirsten replied with relief. "I've not exactly been in luxury accommodation."

"I can't even imagine," Elyse said, ushering Gabe into the washroom to deposit Kirsten next to the tub and closing the door firmly behind him. His absence left a physical pain in Kirsten's chest. She sighed, feeling ever so slightly like a drama queen, as Elyse giggled sympathetically, "I know exactly how you feel! Adrian has exactly the same effect on me. When he is close, the entire world is simply perfect. And when I can't see him, it's like a massive gash through my soul."

"Massive," Kirsten agreed. "How did you and Adrian meet?"

"Well...the first time I saw him, he was dressed in rags, sitting on the ground at the mouth of Harbour City Central Station tunnel playing the flute. And one moment in his company changed my life forever. He did trick me into thinking he was blind and stalked me across a country or two before we actually spoke."

"Nice," Kirsten smiled. "They have a way of making you forget your priorities."

"So true," Elyse replied. "But without Adrian's help, I would have probably been killed up on Far Mountain and my research would have died with me. The Saurians...those reptiles you just met... had obviously followed me up there. I was actually in the middle of jumping off the side of the mountain when Adrian swooped in for possibly the most magical and exciting moment of my life."

"You're a researcher?" Kirsten asked. Something was sparking in her motor cortex and she felt power returning to her limbs. What a relief. It would make her ablutions a much less embarrassing thing.

She had known immediately that Elyse was no ordinary girl. They were kindred spirits. It had to be beyond a coincidence that both girls were working on the solution to the global catastrophe that had befallen their world.

Whereas she was studying the history of the ancient and long forgotten battle between the Guardians and the reptiles from beyond the stars, trying to determine if anything learned from the encounter could help in the current situation, Elyse was attacking the problem from an interesting and unexpected perspective. Plants. That plants had been instrumental in the victory over the reptiles had never crossed Kirsten's mind. She had assumed they were merely ornamental embellishments in the story book she had studied and it was the beams of light which held the power of the Guardians.

The girls compared notes and it was Elyse's turn to be surprised.

"Purple light?" She exclaimed, flushing a little as she remembered the moment in the cabin. "Yes, I've seen it!

Or at least I think I have. Once, when Adrian was close to me. It felt hazy and..."

"Foggy?" Kirsten prompted.

"Yes exactly. Foggy and soft."

Kirsten sat even straighter. "I believe the Guardians harness the light in some way to give them power. When I first saw Gabe, he was saving a homeless man from one of those Saurians. At first there was a soft purple glow, then a bright beam of purple light that came with him as he swooped in. It was intense and unlike anything I've ever witnessed."

Elyse sat thoughtfully on the bathroom stool. Was it even conceivable that this war was being fought on three fronts? The visible (if only to few), macroscopic battles between the Saurians and the Guardians. The microscopic attack by the tiny grey lizard creatures, the plague, that had spread across the entire world and was even now thought to be only an infection. An attack that she had been able to stop in her own body with a fragment of dried plant and a Liroon grasshopper working together for an antidote. And the third battle. Light. Photons. The grey blasters against the violet purple beams of the Guardians.

And the plant! The damaged plant, eaten by the insect, had glowed purple too. What was the significance of the light? Was it the vibrations of the wavelength or the particles it consisted of that affected the parasites so strongly. How she wished her PhD was in Quantum Physics and not Botany.

Elyse looked at Kirsten, happy that the other girl had regained some of her movement and balance. It had been so difficult watching her struggle. It was a horrific side effect of the infection that survivors continued to suffer. Few were able to maintain meaningful lives and she was impressed at how Kirsten had been able to continue her work.

A thought materialized in Elyse's brain. What if the infection was ongoing? What if the tiny lizards were still in her body? Living on her axons, sapping her power, building their little structures from her cells and breeding there. What if there was a cure for this brave and determined girl?

It was worth a try. Elyse called Gabe and as he was carrying Kirsten back to the living room, she hurried over to Adrian's side. He looked at her serious gaze questioningly.

"I have an idea," she whispered to him. "We don't have access to a body scanner, but I strongly suspect that Kirsten's body is still carrying a live colony. Possibly on her spinal cord. I think that may be why she can't move. She is so strong willed and driven that she is able to subdue them somehow, briefly, when her adrenaline increases, and her brain is obviously unaffected, they haven't invaded it yet. I think it may be possible to treat her. We could spare one of our leaves, create a serum and inject it directly into her blood stream."

Adrian nodded. He was thinking of not only Kirsten, but also Gabe. He had seen how close his brother had become to the young woman and how he ached in sympathy with the torture her body was putting her through. And if the serum worked, then hope increased for the other humans in the New World.

"How can I help?" he offered.

"Well, we will have to create a fluid, the same way I did with the dehydrated specimens, but with a tiny segment of leaf material. If you could find the tubing in my bag and a sterile jar, I will boil some water."

Elyse knelt at the growing box and gently snipped a single leaf from the plants who continued to grow at a surprising rate. Some were showing buds.

Soon the pot was steaming into the tubing and condensing, to drip into the jar as pure distilled water. It was an old-fashioned but effective carrier for the thoroughly muddled leaf fragments. Emerald green liquid resulted. The tiniest fragment of the original leaf with the organic residue completed the mixture. All she had to do now was test it.

The obsessive scientist in Elyse bubbled with excitement as she drew up a syringe full of serum. Could this simplest concoction free her new friend of the prison she was condemned to?

"What does Kirsten think about being injected with a green smoothie?" Adrian joked as he leaned over the small jar.

Elyse flushed with guilt over her single-minded quest for a cure. She hadn't even thought of that. What if Kirsten didn't want to take the risk? What if she said no?

Only the end result had been on Elyse's mind. Perhaps the fact that Kirsten really had no hope otherwise, her struggle had only one outcome. A frightfully difficult death. This perhaps gave her no choice. She had been too preoccupied and selfish to consider the other girl's feelings. Adrian smiled as he saw the thoughts chasing across Elyse's expressive features. He gave her hand a reassuring squeeze and pulled her to her feet.

"Come on. I'm sure she'll love the idea. How could she not?"

Adrian was right. Barely able to believe what she was hearing, Kirsten beamed as she agreed to being the first trial subject for Elyse's revolutionary serum. Gabe looked worried as he sat beside her with his arm wrapped around her slim shoulders. Since finding her, was it only a few hours ago, he could not imagine existence without her. Kirsten felt his arm tighten around her and leaned gratefully into his strength.

"If it works, what can I expect, and how soon?" she wanted to know.

Elyse hesitated. She wanted to tell her friend that she believed the serum would clear the creatures from her body swiftly, as it did for her, leaving her body to slowly recover and rebuild its tissues, but she didn't want to raise Kirsten's hopes too high. With neural involvement, things would surely be more complicated and fraught with variables.

She settled for a quick shrug and a non-committal scientific mumble. In any case, that was enough for Kirsten who held up a shaky, pale arm, palm up, ready for the injection. "To victory over these hideous little beasts! Here goes nothing!" she laughed weakly. The momentary strength she had been feeling was already starting to fade and her breathing was becoming a little laboured.

Tears sprang into Gabe's eyes. Giving him a quick glance, Elyse found herself becoming slightly misty too. She wiped her eyes surreptitiously and approached with the green juice filled syringe.

It was a solemn moment. Everyone knew it could turn out to be a momentous occasion that would turn the tide of the microscopic invasion. Adrian and Cam stood quietly behind her as Elyse gently inserted the needle into Kirsten's bluish vein and allowed the liquid to slowly enter her bloodstream. She kept holding the frail arm for a long moment, willing some dramatic result. A return to strength, to power.

Everyone held their breath, waiting.

Kirsten's smile slowly faded as nothing happened for long minutes. She looked into Gabe's brown eyes noticing they weren't brown, but shot through with purple. They began to glow, a deep amethyst light that seared across the space between them and into her very soul. She began to feel a tingling from her elbow upwards to her neck which quickly intensified into a burning heat that ran over every nerve in her body. She gasped and arched backwards as her brain felt like a violet wildfire had taken hold there.

Dimly aware of those around her asking questions, she was lost in the electrical storm taking place deep inside. The creatures within were not giving up without a fight. She closed her eyes and was almost able to see the microscopic battle taking place. The green liquid was swirling, shot through with vivid purple. It seemed to be defending her against the grey creatures which had turned her body into their playground. She could almost see her own nerves flowering brightly again in the rubble of her cells. Her brain had connected telepathically to her body and she felt it expanding with knowledge and light.

And then it was over. Complete silence. No pain. She took a deep breath and opened made fists with her hands then stretched them out. Unobstructed and free. Oxygen flooded her lungs. Maybe she had died. Kirsten opened her eyes gingerly. The room was still there. Elyse was standing over her as she had been seconds ago, holding her breath as were the Guardians. She turned to the dear man beside her, marvelling at how easily her body moved, and tears of joy streamed down her cheeks.

Not able to believe it, he looked at her intently, his eyes still vivid, and she nodded vigorously, not able to speak through the happiness that she felt. He spun her around and hugged her tightly, burying his face in her hair. She slid her arms around his waist and pressed ever closer.

Kirsten could possibly have chosen this moment to go on forever.

But, it couldn't of course. They were not ordinary people, living ordinary lives. She had discovered the truth about a coming invasion and been the second successful participant in a trial for a means to defend every single person in the New World. He had wings and flew around on purple beams with his brothers vanquishing evil reptiles! Her new friend was a genius scientist who had cooked up a cure for the plague of a lifetime. Together, they had a world to save.

Reluctantly she released her grip and slid her hands to Gabe's face, lifting it to hers and kissing him fiercely the way she had always wanted to before pushing herself away. He let her go and instead of drooping like a withered weed, she straightened and reached both arms above her head.

"So, this is what it feels like!" she said, breathing deeply again and stretched like a cat after a long nap. Turning to Elyse, she said, somewhat unnecessarily, "it worked!"

Elyse exhaled, the tension sliding away and being replaced by relief and effervescent bubbles of joy. It was quite a spectacular result and way more dramatic than she could have wished for. But now there was so much work to be done.

The active factor needed to be synthesised and reproduced on a massive scale. Her findings, carefully redacted to protect Far Mountain, needed to not only be presented to her team leader and then the Infection Mitigation Council, but needed to be accepted by the people of all five cities, and quickly, before the Saurians could mount a counter offensive.

The volume of work ahead of her seemed insurmountable and she decided to just leave the thinking to tomorrow and give in to the happiness around her, just for tonight. Turning to her equipment, she pulled out her electromyography equipment and ran tests on Kirsten's nerve tissue. It was recovering at a remarkable rate, but her muscle fibres were following more slowly. The wasting was extensive and global throughout her body. Even her heart and lungs were weak. All the smooth muscle of her internal organs was thin and sluggish. They needed to be rebuilt cell by cell. They needed fuel.

As if echoing her musings, Kirsten groaned, "I am so hungry, can't even remember being so famished. Sorry to spoil this epic moment, but do you have anything to eat here?"

The guardians laughed. Food was something they definitely had enough of. It took a lot of sustenance to keep flying. It was an energy absorbing exercise at best, but adding some fights to it made them super hungry too.

"Leave it to us," Cam replied as he and Adrian began preparing a feast. Taking a look at Gabe and Kirsten, still cuddling on the couch, Elyse laughed too and went to join them. It was quite relaxing to sit on a stool and watch their choreographed movements, chopping, sizzling, tossing. Adrian slid a glass of juice across the counter to her with a practiced flourish and she sipped it quietly, smiling and listening to their brotherly banter.

She would have been a lot less relaxed if she had seen Mara and her army of Saurians poring through Kirsten's research until they found the story book that detailed exactly how the Guardians had defeated them in the first war. They growled with satisfaction as they handed the old and well-read book to their leader and sat in a circle around her as she read each page to them in a bizarre parody of kindergarteners listening to their teacher.

When she came to the page detailing the battle, she lifted the book up and showed them the place where their species had been subdued. Far Mountain. Tongues collectively flicked in an out in anticipation. Far Mountain had to be destroyed, along with all the people who lived in its shadow. When they were ready for the final attack, there would be no chance that the winged defenders would even have a home base.

CHAPTER 19

The early morning breakfast had a completely different atmosphere. There was so much to do. Papers were opened up across the table and everyone ate absently as they discussed the plan for defending against the imminent attack. Serum had to be synthesised, and quickly. This had to remain a secret project but needed to be opened up to the scholars, scientists and technicians of the entire New World.

Elyse had to return to work and face the destruction of her lab as well as the curiosity of her workmates. She had to share her specimens and her medical history. As soon as the active properties were isolated, her team leader would distribute their findings to other labs and hence to the serum manufacturers. The Infection Mitigation Council had to be informed as well. This was a trickier situation, as so many differing opinions on the cause of the plague had created chaos in the leadership.

And then the final piece of the puzzle, the purple light, had to be added with each dose. There was no way a handful of Guardians could do this for all five cities. They needed help. They needed to consult with the Far

Mountain elders. How had the mountain been able to help during the first battle? Was it just a fairy tale that it had opened up or had it been a coincidental volcanic eruption?

It was decided that Gabe and Kirsten would travel there and investigate while Adrian and Elyse worked on the serum.

The girls went into Elyse's room to find Kirsten some travelling clothes. The amulet, still attached to the sash, sparkled in the light.

"I found this in the grass on the side of the mountain. I don't know how long it was up there, or who left it for me to find but it brought me safely home. I'd like you to have it." She fastened it to Kirsten's cloak and wiped a tear from her cheek as she farewelled her new found friend.

Cam would contact the rest of the Dark Guardians who would keep the Saurians off balance with as many attacks as they could muster. Still continuing to work in the shadows they would have to keep the operation covert, for the time being anyway. At some stage the humans of the New World would have to finally experience the true nature of the planet they had settled with such hopes for peace.

Cam grinned wickedly to himself as he anticipated the fun that he could have, especially when the secret of Far

Mountain and its Guardians came out and he could just let loose on every reptile that came his way without ever worrying about being seen again. His eyes glowed a savage purple as imagined the grey slime spraying all over the ground and oozing into the depths.

Gripping his knife handle as he sprang from his chair, Cam tucked the rest of his breakfast into his mouth and chewed happily as he said his goodbyes to his newly paired up and never again to be free brothers. He felt the wind rushing across his face in the dawn glow as his wings unfurled and took him high into the sky.

He would have a lot of flying to do before daylight. There were nine other Guardian houses in the city, each with three or four Guardians. His favourite was a girl called Rose. She was aloof and didn't know he existed but he didn't mind. She was a strong warrior, and single minded. On occasion he had seen a tiny grin on her fierce face as she had vanquished a Saurian and watched it disintegrate into slime. It was that grin that enchanted him most. They were kindred spirits, and one day, when the job was done, and the last invader had been destroyed never to return, he would ask her for a sparring match back home at Far Mountain.

A voice inside his head told him she would probably defeat him, but he grinned harder. Maybe she wouldn't.

They would have so many laughs together reminiscing about their adventures in the New World.

He turned towards the ground and dove to the first Guardian house. Despite the early hour, everyone was awake. Rose was sharpening her blades, instantly alert as he flew through the door and folded his wings silently.

She didn't smile, only nodded briefly at his greeting as did the others. He nodded back, not able to keep his own smile quite hidden.

His news bought concrete intention where there had been only bravery and hope against impossible odds. With it came excitement as the men and women of the Guardians assembled and prepared for battle. Soon all the houses had been informed, weapons sharpened and the silent war commenced.

CHAPTER 20

Elyse fidgeted in the centre of the gathering, nervous as always speaking to her peers before launching into a detailed account of her infection, solution, travels, meetings with the Guardians and the elders of Far Mountain, and finally of the combination of factors which had forged the ultimate cure. Her colleagues, usual reticence forgotten, clapped loudly as she completed her account. Her team leader patted her on the shoulder and congratulated her on a job well started. As the re-opened lab sprang into action the team leader contacted his counterparts in other parts of the city. Work on the serum began in earnest.

Elyse shrugged apologetically at Adrian. She had so much to do that there was no time to spend with him. He would be so bored. His brothers and friends fiercely battled the enemy, while he stood guard. He gave no indication of anything but calm patience as he leant nonchalantly against a wall and watched everyone in motion around him. An island of stillness in the midst of frenetic scientific activity. Finally, she stopped worrying about him and began to work.

The grasshopper variable was puzzling her, was it just the purple glow that was affecting the molecules in the plant, or was there something else at play. She didn't have long to wonder. Her high-powered microscope magnified the chewed edges of the plant, still faintly illuminated but also sprinkled with a purple crystalline substance that wavered before her eyes and slowly changed the plant fibres into crystals too.

Scraping some of the crystals to one side, Elyse increased the magnification and noticed the sharp, curving structure of the minerals, and the way they moved, sided to side, like scythes whipping across her line of sight. She gasped with the significance of the miniature weapons and hurried to the freezer where she had stored the powdery residue of the sliver of skin that she had shaved off her arm was it only a few weeks ago? It was one of the few things that had escaped the Saurian rampage.

Placing a few flakes onto the slide, she was impressed but not surprised to see the glowing crystals increase their waving motion and grow towards the grey powder until they had literally chopped it into pieces and engulfed it. Like a microscopic army, they had overcome their foe, and, when no longer needed, had become inert again. She placed her finger close to them on the slide and they started to wave, ever so gently and glowed brightly. So beautiful. Purple, shot through with deeper purple, white and clear streaks.

"Adrian," take a look at this, she motioned to him, "have you seen anything like this before?"

As he came close, she pulled back from the microscope just slightly, just enough to be able to feel his warmth as he bent over the microscope aperture. She looked at his eye as he peered at her discovery. Yes, she knew it! His eyes were the exact shade of purple as the crystals. Just as she realised that he was in some way connected to the crystals, to the light, Adrian looked up, his eyes glowing just slightly and nodded. "They're amethyst crystals. The same ones we find on the slopes of Far Mountain. They are very precious to my people. Sacred almost. Each one is unique. I've never seen any this small before of course. And I have never seen them moving! They are incredible."

Elyse smiled at him. "They are what I've been looking for, Adrian. They are part of the Liroon and, I suspect, help them digest the plants by cutting the fibrous leaves into smaller, more digestible pieces. But, more than that, when I placed some parasite residue near them, they moved towards it, churned it into pieces until it became part of the crystal itself."

"Impressive," Adrian mused.

"Exactly what I thought! It is like the crystals are attacking and destroying the infection with intent. Which could mean that they are alive."

"And able to differentiate between friend and foe?" Adrian asked.

"Possibly. I think that it is all connected. The very rock of Far Mountain, all the plants and animals that live there, even the Guardians themselves. All connected by the amethyst crystals. The light that glows from the tiniest fragment is exactly the same colour as the flashes in your eyes Adrian, and it is the hazy glow I see when you are close to me and I start to feel..." Elyse tried to find the words to describe the emotions she experienced in his presence, but could only manage to touch his forearm and smile at him. It was enough, because he nodded with understanding.

"A purple beam forms to help us when we are in the midst of battle. It is said that it came from deep within the Mountain when the Saurians first invaded from beyond the stars to strengthen us and is the magic thread that connects all."

"Adrian, I knew you weren't a Dark Guardian. You are not dark in any way. You are a defender of this world and even if you must do such dark things, you are the light. You are an Amethyst Guardian." Elyse slid her arms around his waist and held him as tightly as she could. And now she could feel the light that glowed between them with her mind. Even she was now connected to him, through the crystals that had become part of her when she fought of the infection. They belonged to each other, now and forever.

Lost in her epic realization, Elyse didn't hear her team leader until he had cleared his throat for a third time and even then, she had trouble concentrating on his excited fast words.

He had managed to contact the Medical Director of the IMC who had initialized preparations for mass producing serum, other labs had begun analysing the active components of the alpine plant specimens Elyse had distributed. A quantum physics professor was on his way with equipment to study the wavelength of the light and interpret its significance.

"There's something else," Elyse waved him over to her microscope.

"What the...?" he exclaimed when he peered into it.

"Put your finger on the slide," she instructed and then laughed as her unflappable team leader jerked his head back and gulped loudly. "This is it!" he almost shouted as he found his voice again. "This is the weapon we've been looking for. This will turn the tide on this terrible plague and free our people of the pain and suffering they've been enduring"

His excitement travelled around the lab and soon everyone was taking turns looking through the microscope at the bristling crystals.

Elyse motioned for the scientists to gather around her, even as she spoke, she marvelled at how her shyness had just vanished in the wake of the importance of the information she had to share. These people were more than just colleagues, they were friends.

"This is a momentous discovery," she said to them. "It means so much more than any of us has realised. These crystals will not only be our salvation, they will become part of us. And we, in turn will become part of this planet. We will be connected to every living thing here and even the rocks beneath our feet. These crystals came from the depths of Far Mountain a very, very long time ago in the distant past, when a vicious alien race of reptilians called the Saurians landed on this planet and tried to overrun the peaceful inhabitants of Homeland.

Their ancestors made the decision to move beyond the past and forget it so they could live without fear and when we colonised New World, we also lived without fear, but we live in ignorance. A friend of mine found a children's story book of legends. It showed Far Mountain with a massive opening. Great beams of purple light were erupting from it and giving the Guardians of our planet the strength to subdue the invaders and send them deep underground. Forgotten but not quite dead. They are planning another attack. I believe this parasitic plague is the first wave. And I believe the crystal serum we will make can stop them from destroying us at a microscopic level. We can work together to strengthen every human while Guardians repel the larger Saurians and banish them from both the New World and Far Mountain forever."

Her words echoed into silence as her workmates grasped the significance of her words. The world they had known had changed in an instant with the new knowledge she had shared. It had become both richer and more terrifying than they could ever have imagined. And once they knew, the reassuring life of ignorance they had existed in would never be an option again. The quest for a cure had become a race to prevent the destruction of everything they knew and loved. Their world was at stake.

With renewed enthusiasm they separated to their various workstations and she was left alone with Adrian again.

"You know, I didn't even realise what it all meant until you spoke just then," he remarked thoughtfully.

"Neither did I. Only when I hugged you a minute ago and felt our connection deep inside, did the puzzle pieces start to fit. It is just something we Earthers haven't had much experience with. We made a real mess of our planet, so many species extinct and with each one we all became poorer. When we found New World, we pledged never to destroy natural life, but we thought we could accomplish that by isolating ourselves from it. We never imagined the richness of a life that was entwined with everything around us. Can you even imagine? Of course, you can, it's how you live!" Elyse flushed and looked down, "I'm so sorry, I'm babbling."

Adrian took her gently by the shoulders and held her close again. "It's true, but I have never felt as close to anything or anyone in this world as I feel to you."

Elyse relaxed into his arms for a moment before reluctantly turning towards her microscope again.

Out of the corner of her eye she saw Adrian stiffen and whirl around to the door before it exploded into a thousand shards. He had pulled his knife from its scabbard and ran towards it before she had even moved.

Saurians burst over the remnants of the door, grey photons blasting out of their ugly weapons. Several scientists fell screaming as they were hit. Elyse instinctively dropped to the ground and crawled under her desk. Her specimen! It was on the microscope slide. She couldn't allow it to be taken. Despite the flashes of light around her, she reached her hand up and carefully extracted it from its clips and tucked it into her pocket before burrowing even deeper under the desk.

She could hear sounds of fighting. Grunts of anger and pain as one after another of the Saurians fell around her and disintegrated into slimy grey ooze. The flashes became less frequent and then stopped altogether.

"Elyse!"

She heard Adrian calling her and bumped her head on the desk as she struggled to get up. He was covered in grey dust and his worried frown dissolved into relief as he saw her emerge from her hiding place.

The lab was yet again a scene of chaos and destruction. Elyse's workmates lay groaning on the floor or wandered, confused and vacant. No one was dead thankfully and even though she couldn't be sure, she didn't think anything had been taken.

"They were after you," Adrian told her as he closed the gap between them again. "Mara and her minions. She got away. They didn't." He couldn't keep the satisfaction out of his voice. He finally felt what Gabe had always felt when he killed them. Nothing but satisfaction. The regret he had always felt was gone. Any feelings of remorse had vanished when they tried to harm Elyse. When they had attacked thousands of innocent humans using their microscopic army and left them struggling to survive. He had still felt guilty every time he took a life but when they had threatened this one small woman, he had felt such fear and rage that he had killed them all with nothing but cold hatred.

Elyse nodded, not quite able to keep the shakiness out of her voice. "I could see them as they fell. I don't think they had time to take our research."

"No," he answered, "but I am going to take you all somewhere safe now, somewhere they won't be able to find you when they regroup." Adrian turned to the scientists who were slowly getting up and ordered them to collect as much equipment as they could as quickly as possible because it was time to move out.

No one argued with him. Luckily his apartment was large enough for a crowd. He and his brothers had never had a party before, now was as good a time as any to start. Some food and drinks would go a long way to restoring Elyse's workmates to their usual scholastic demeanour.

He pulled the team leader aside and advised him to let the other labs know that the Saurians were no longer hiding in the shadows but prepared to abandon their disguises and attack anyone who stood in the way of their plans for domination. The other man nodded gravely. The shock of the attack had momentarily dislodged his calm confidence but he was regaining it rapidly. Finally, he would be able to make a difference in the world and help so many of the people he had been helpless to assist before. There was important work to be done and he was ready.

After packing their equipment and notes hurriedly, taking separate transports, everyone from the lab joined Adrian and Elyse in his apartment. There was an amazing atmosphere in the huge great room, half party, half panic but all business.

Adrian leant in the doorway watching them. Again, he had nothing to do.

Once in a while, Elyse would look up from her work and smile at him. She was so relieved that even though the future was uncertain, she was no longer helpless and no longer alone in her quest. Her smile turned into a frown as she saw Cam quietly entering the apartment, it seemed moments later, but could have been hours.

Adrian's perpetually happy brother was uncharacteristically grim. He ignored the scientists completely. As the brothers spoke, Adrian's expression sharpened and intensified. He looked at Elyse again and her heart sank. Something terrible had happened. Leaving her work station, she joined them questioningly.

"The lab has now been completely destroyed. They are searching for us. It's only a matter of time. The other Guardians are fighting battles on all fronts."

"Oh no!" she cried. "Not yet, we are nowhere near ready!"

Adrian walked over to the floor to ceiling windows and looked into the apricot dawn light. Dread filled him as he spotted Sky-flyers hovering over a plume of smoke that rose above the city line and hung over what was left of the lab. Mara had not wasted any time.

The Sky-flyers darted then hovered in a search pattern over the tall buildings. There was nothing to lead them to this building, but they would be able to sense anyone who had been there. It was no longer safe anywhere. It was time to say goodbye to the view. Adrian looked up at the cornice of the room where a small button flashed and stared at it intently until it stopped flashing. Solid shutters emerged from the ceiling and slid slowly over the windows, turning the building from a showpiece of design into an impenetrable fortress.

He became aware of Elyse standing beside him when her hand slid into his. The last of the morning light disappeared from view.

"You have to go, don't you?" she asked quietly. "You need to slow them down while we complete the serum and distribute it. The Guardians need you now. And when we succeed, we will have a lifetime together."

Adrian smiled sadly at her optimism and nodded. She was right. He could only stand and watch here. Out there he had a vicious and overwhelming enemy to fight. There were so few Guardians. And yet it was agony to leave her unprotected. He bent his head and kissed her desperately before tearing himself away. He knew that if he had stayed one more moment, he would have changed his mind.

Elyse stood, feeling bereft, as Adrian and Cam strode out. The two men ran up the steps to the roof and without hesitation flew into the ever-brightening sky.

CHAPTER 21

Gabe had never enjoyed the Sky Rail as much as he did with Kirsten by his side. She was full of happiness and wonder. Everything was new and exciting to her. Even being able to sit upright and look out of the window was a fresh experience.

They arrived at Gabe's hometown on sunset. The magic of deep turquoise, embroidered with flowers was even more intense with the multicoloured sky glow. Kirsten gasped at the beauty around her and stumbled as she stepped off the platform. Gabe caught her easily and laughed. She wasn't used to balancing on her feet, let alone walking and looking around. She laughed with him and whirled around to face him. The scenery could wait, her need to be ever closer to him could not. Pulling his head down, she kissed him. It was meant to be a quick kiss, but somewhere along the line they completely forgot that plan and didn't remember reality until they heard a chuckle beside them.

Drawing apart, they were met with the amused grin of Gabe's father Constantine. "Aren't you going to introduce me, son?" he prompted. "You must be Kirsten. Welcome to Homeland."

Kirsten loved him on sight and leant over for a hug. Gabe hugged them both.

Looking over Constantine's shoulder, Kirsten caught her first glimpse of Far Mountain. It loomed over the small town and was so much bigger and more magnificent than any picture could convey. The men followed her gaze and nodded at their mountain gravely. It was their protector, the source of their strength and identity.

"Come," said Constantine, wrapping around each of their shoulders. "Let us go home. Dokkia has dinner on the table and is eager to meet you, Kirsten."

Gabe's parents' house was modest and cosy, nestled into a fragrant garden, festooned with flowering vines. Fireflies illuminated the winding path to the front door which was open. A warm glow shone out into the gathering gloom. It was a storybook setting, and one Kirsten had never thought she would be part of. Gabe's mother met them at the door with more hugs and laughter."

Kirsten thought that if this was what family was like, then she really had suffered an unimaginable loss being an orphan.

The table was groaning under a feast of vegetable and grain dishes. Fruits on raised platters studded with large nuts and flowers formed the centrepiece. Candles flickered here and there. There was more freshness here than Kirsten had eaten in her entire life. Pure happiness filled her as she ate and drank and listened to Gabe recount how he had fallen in love with her instantly, and how she had been on the forefront of the fight against the Saurian invaders with her research and bravery against all odds.

She slept fitfully in a strange bed, listening to the unfamiliar country sounds and worrying about the morning but finally drifted off at dawn.

Broad daylight streaming through the windows woke her. Stretching, she luxuriated in the unfamiliar feeling of being able to move any time she wanted to. The softness of the pillow caressing her cheek, the crisp coolness of the sheets. She would never take her body for granted. Or the marvellous feeling of being loved, of being part of a family. But she couldn't stay here forever, basking in the sunshine, there was so much to do before anyone could rest.

Gabe and his father had already left to gather the Guardians and ready them for battle. The communication barrier web far above them would be reinforced tenfold. Only a chosen Web Guardian knew the location of the control panels and Gabe had told her that no one knew who it was.

Dokkia was outside, a halo of sunshine around her flowing silver hair, surrounded by snowy white farm birds who gathered at her feet for treats. It was an idyllic scene and Kirsten stood for several minutes, entranced. The older woman must have sensed her presence and turned towards her smiling and waving gently at the birds. "My girls have provided us with a magnificent breakfast. Let us go in and enjoy their gifts. Since he retired from being a Guardian, Constantine has become such a very good chef that I seldom have the opportunity to cook," she laughed.

And it was magnificent. Herbal omelettes washed down with glorious, cerise fruit juice. Kirsten was beginning to feel stronger and more alive than she had even been. Afterwards they walked down to the town and made their way to the meeting place where a crowd had already gathered. Most people were farmers, wearing simply made pale clothes, which made the Dark Guardians even more startling in contrast. Dokkia remarked she had never seen so many in one place. She was relieved to have Gabe close, but Kirsten could tell she worried about her other sons. Fighting an implacable enemy in the cold greyness of Harbour City.

Kirsten sat close to Dokkia and held her hand, also worried about her new friends. Who knew what they were enduring at this very moment.

CHAPTER 22

Adrian soared high above the city catching a thermal draft, as he counted the Sky-flyers jagging and darting below. So far there were only five. He signalled to Cam as they flew closer. They would target each flyer as a team, coming up behind the flyers together, then splitting up at the last second, aiming for the far side wings where the Saurian pilots' visibility was lowest.

Each craft was larger than a human, but it lacked ease and manoeuvrability. The Guardians had learnt to use its own power and momentum against it.

The first hit was a surprise for the enemy who had no time to react. Each brother grasped a wing tip and swirled a flyer out of balance up and in towards its neighbour, so they swung closer, collided and crashed into the harbour. Another flyer had lagged behind and was also an easy target. The last three were ready. In attack formation, they filled the air with grey photon blasts. The Guardians evaded the clumsier mechanical flyers with the flexibility of their bodies and wings.

Between the buildings they flew, tilting sideways then diving steeply towards the ground, so when the next flyer tried to follow, it couldn't pull up and slammed into the street below. The explosion sent streams of glass shards from the surrounding windows, impaling the lizard like creatures as they tried to crawl from the wreckage of their craft while motors slowly throbbed to a stop. Adrian and Cam paused, hovering, waiting for the remaining flyers. They were met by only silence and the whistle of high-altitude winds.

There was no time to waste, they could not let the enemy escape and bring reinforcements yet again. The Guardians hoped that a major deployment had not yet happened. As they ascended, the pale twin Jet streams of the flyers became visible. As one, the brothers turned towards their quarry and gave chase. This time they needed to take down both flyers at once. It was a manoeuvre they had practiced as apprentice Guardians above the orchards of Homeland. Adrian took the outside wing of the flyer on the right, and Cam mirrored his moves, they swung across the flyers' nose cones and then let go, flying swiftly upwards as the flyers helplessly crashed headlong into each other and disintegrated into grey dust that rained harmlessly onto the city below.

Breathing deeply, they ascended, until the rising sun caught their wings and turned the world into a glittering golden orb around them before gliding down gently, giving themselves time to catch their breath before they reached home. Cam's grin had returned. Of all the many things he loved to do, flying at sunrise topped the list. Besting an enemy with superior numbers was possibly a close second, he reckoned. He looked at Adrian to catch that now familiar scowl Adrian wore every time he was separated from Elyse. His grin widened. Being a couple must be something else. But there was no way he was giving up his freedom for anyone.

But as he watched Adrian and Elyse reuniting moments later, his resolve wavered slightly. They were both usually reserved people. In trying to keep their joy harnessed and inconspicuous they were both awkward and achingly sweet. He turned away and busied himself making coffee.

Scientists were sleeping soundly in all corners of the room. They had worked throughout the night and needed more sleep, but now was not the time for rest. Not until the serum was complete.

CHAPTER 23

An uncomfortable silence had fallen over the gathering as Gabe and Kirsten stood before them. The unspoken rule to avoid contact with outsiders had been broken, and broken in the most public of ways. Once again, one of their Dark Guardians had arrived with a woman, not of their kind. And once again, she was extraordinary.

Whereas they had maintained that ignoring the past, a simple life and adherence to strict rules of non-interference would keep them safe to the point of being apathetic in the face of the suffering the plague had bought their New World counterparts, she had risked her life to bring their equally brave and tragic history to life. They had once all been warriors through necessity and had been victorious against impossible odds. Now all but a few had lost the skills and the very nature to be able to defend their mountain.

If Kirsten was aware of their unease, she gave no sign. She was still having a little trouble coordinating prolonged standing, so once in a while, Gabe had to support her. She recounted the story she had found in the precious children's book so all could hear. When she finished, the silence continued. Most, but not all of her listeners were hearing this story for the first time. The ones who had heard before, nodded their heads slowly.

The time had come to shed their farming implements and take up swords and knives, for the secretly chosen Web Guardian among them to set out alone along the dangerous Sky Pass and into Far Mountain itself to ask for help from the Amethyst fire within.

This person had kept vigil over the mysterious place of power for a lifetime, maintaining the technology of long ago. Chosen by ballot after the first Saurian attack, and then held for as long as they could climb, before teaching the next candidate, the keeper of the Amethyst was a sacred trust.

In any case, the chosen one would not travel alone. It was Dokkia. She waited until her family was safely ensconced in the cottage, hugged Constantine, and told him the truth about herself.

"It has been the hardest task of my life, to keep this from you, my love. Harder than allowing all three of our sons to follow in your footsteps and become Dark Guardians. Harder than facing Sky Pass. But I had no choice. If the Saurians had captured me, I would have ended it swiftly." She pulled a curved blade from the folds of her gown.

"Oh, my darling girl," Constantine sobbed, holding her close. "I knew in my heart that you carried a heavy burden, but I assumed it was worry for our boys. You are so brave, my love."

She sagged against him for a moment. Relief at finally not being alone with her secret left her weakened momentarily. Then she straightened again and Constantine saw his wife as the warrior that she always had been. Her soft kindness was still there, but her strength shone through. Through the dimness in the cottage, he caught sight of Gabe staring at his mother as if he had never seen her before either. He seemed instantly younger and more innocent. More like the child he once had been.

Constantine went over and thumped him on the back. "Well son," he asked, "where do you think you boys got the idea of running all over the planet, vanquishing lizards, came from?"

Gabe face slowly broke into a smile and he strode to his mother, and embraced her tightly. "I won't let you go alone," he vowed.

"Neither will I," echoed Kirsten coming closer. She didn't know how she would cope, climbing a mountain when she had barely started to walk again, but she wasn't letting them go without her. These people were her family now.

"That's settled." Constantine as they all hugged. "We shall make a day of it. Some coffee, I'll pack a picnic basket. You, Kirsten, have not yet tasted my Sweetberry pie."

All in all, it wasn't as terrifying a climb as she had imagined. Constantine unveiled some ornate antler shaped walking poles and Gabe carried a pack with provisions for all of them.

Kirsten was able to stop now and then to fight off dizziness by lying down and taking deep breaths under the deep turquoise, cloudless sky. Gabe and his parents stopped with her, sitting on the soft silvery mountain grass and letting her feel as though she was as strong as any of them. Feeling Elyse's clasp against her stomach as she breathed, Kirsten wondered where the other girl had found the amulet and if it would also bring her safely home again. When she touched it, she felt warmth, power and a strange sense of peace.

Sky Pass was another matter altogether, terrifying was a mild word for it. A narrow ledge between the two peaks of Far Mountain with a sheer cliff on one side and a sheer drop on the other which hummed with whirling winds, Sky Pass was an impossible walk. Just getting close to it caused Kirsten to wobble on her newly functional legs as isolated muscle fibres twitched uncontrollably. Her brain said no, quite insistently and stopped her forward motion.

Constantine and Dokkia looked at her with concern. She knew that she had become pale and ready to faint. How frustrating. She was holding them back with her weaknesses both physical and psychological. For a second, she didn't even feel Gabe's gentle hand on her shoulder until he turned her towards him and lifted her chin so the world shrank to just the wonder of his purple eyes.

"Hey," he said with a quiet smile, "have you forgotten something?"

She shook her head. "I don't think so...what is it?"

"This," he laughed, sliding his arms around her waist as his wings unfurled behind him. And, as she gasped, not having a chance to even react, he rose from the ground and hovered above the ground. "Falling is not an option."

Still holding her against him, his eyes never leaving hers, he flew slowly over the pass. As he reached the rocky path of the other side, he started to set her down, but her knees were still threatening to give way. Gabe held her close even after her strength returned. It was only when his parents had re-joined them, that he was able to make himself let her go. She felt herself blushing a little from embarrassment but when she looked at Constantine and

Dokkia, she was relieved to see that they were concentrating on the path ahead.

Kirsten's awful, low-pressure dizziness had given way to euphoria and the light headedness of pure relief. Her legs had decided to cooperate again, now that they weren't actually needed as much. She playfully pushed Gabe away and smiled, "I will remember that for next time."

But he didn't smile back. His eyes were serious as he looked ahead to where his parents were. "We are no longer alone," he said with foreboding.

Kirsten felt a chill run over her skin. Several seconds later, she felt a vibration through her feet which became the steady throb of a Sky-flyer. She turned to Gabe questioningly, but he was no longer beside her. She gasped as she watched him soar into the air. His wings glistened in the sunlight as he stopped and turned towards the sound of the Sky-flyer. It was beyond the protruding cave face. With a quick look down at Kirsten, then his mother and father, Gabe shot towards the sound and out of view.

Without wasting any more time, Kirsten started to run towards his parents with all the grace of a new born calf. Her feet didn't want to cooperate, but she forced herself to keep going and at some stage, her brain must have accessed a memory of running. From feeling like she was wading through a dream, she felt the wind rushing towards her as she raced down the path. They had been turned waiting for her, but as they saw how quickly she was catching up, they faced towards their destination and began hurrying.

Gabe caught up with them just before they reached the cave entrance. He looked completely nonchalant, as if he had just been for a relaxed stroll.

Just a tiny sliver of darkness between the rocks. Nothing that could have signified an opening to what transpired to be an antechamber. Its walls were dimly lit by thousands of pin point lights of phosphorescence. Glow threads. The group had little time to marvel at the tiny creatures who had found their way to this cold and inhospitable place as they walked carefully across the cave floor to the far end. It was just solid rock. A dead end. Kirsten only had time to feel a tinge of disappointment that this was the wrong cave before Dokkia opened her arms wide and beseeched the mountain for help.

Before their eyes the wall dissolved and a massive modern room became visible on the other side. The glare of artificial lights shocked their every sense. A hologram of a net hovered above them. A ring of instruments which rumbled softly below the net drew their attention. Even to their untrained eyes, everything looked in perfect working order. Elyse would have loved this place.

It was the planetary defence system, explained Dokkia as she adjusted the parameters to increase the power of the shield above. She would periodically check and maintain the equipment without fully understanding how it functioned. She knew that it kept the Saurians trapped on this planet with no way to summon reinforcements.

Completely out of place in this technologically advanced masterpiece, an ancient door at the far end of the room led to yet another puzzle. Etched figures adorned the granite of the door. The silver of the ornate handle sparkled in the bright light.

"Oh no," Dokkia said, "this door has always been open. What we need is on the other side."

Constantine took hold of the handle and tried to draw it back. It was no use. The door would not move. There were no visible hinges or lock. Nothing to give any indication of how to pass through to the other side. The older couple looked around for anything in the cave which might help.

Kirsten walked up to the door and placed her hand on the smooth cool surface of the polished stone. It was magnificent. She ran her fingers over the brightly lit etchings, embedded here and there with gems. It was like a carved story book, she thought. That's it! It was the story told in the story book she had uncovered. Someone with an incredible talent had made this long ago. As she interpreted the etchings and came to the great battle, her fingers encountered a gap in the story, a piece worn away as if by time itself. If she hadn't studied the fairy tale, she would have missed it. Oval in shape, and about the size of her palm. Could it be this simple?

She reached down, undid the sash around her waist and freed the buckle locked into it. Without giving herself a chance to wonder at the probabilities of her hunch working, she pressed the back of the buckle into the gap. It clicked into place as if made for the door, the jewels glowed and silver sparkled in the light. Taking a deep breath, Kirsten took hold of the handle and the door swung open silently.

A whoosh of warm air escaped from the cave beyond. It was illuminated by an incredible violet glow. A light unlike any she had ever seen. It seemed alive, shimmering as they walked in. At the centre of the huge, roughly hewn octagonal cave a giant amethyst crystal stood, almost touching the ceiling. Light emanated from its many facets, reflecting off the sparkling cave walls. Light and a tangible power that at once filled the space with energy but also with a still calmness of the ages.

Kirsten sighed as she beheld its beauty. She felt Gabe's presence beside her. She reached for his hand and entwined her fingers with his. Looking up at him she found the same look of wonder in his eyes. This was the amethyst he had been unknowingly guarding his whole life.

Movement on the other side of the crystal interrupted the intensity of the moment. It was Dokkia and Constantine. They had placed a tapestry rug onto the floor and were seated on it, holding onto each other tightly. The amethyst seemed to sense their presence, particularly Dokkia's. The shimmers of violet surrounded her like a halo. Slowly, the halo grew to encircle her husband and then increased in both size and luminosity until it enveloped Gabe and Kirsten too. As it did, a million thoughts and memories, images of the skies filled with planets and suns, forests and oceans, people and animals. The history of a thousand worlds, all at once but not at all confronting. The cycle of life in all its glory when seen far enough away to make the inevitable tragedy just a natural progression to the joy beyond.

Kirsten felt tears streaming down her face from the beauty and the knowledge that flooded her mind. She felt strong and capable and well. And then, at once, it was over, and she felt both bereft but also lighter. Her brain had cleared of all the traumas caused by the parasites and the resulting paralysis as well as her attack by the Saurians.

All that remained was strength, determination and concurrence with the thoughts of the people in this cave.

It was enough. As she looked around, she met exactly the same intention gazing back at her. There was an important task at hand and they were ready.

Without having to speak, they picked up their packs and moved out of the cave complex and into the bright sunshine. The Sky-flyers were nowhere to be seen. Only the whistling alpine winds moved across the inhospitable terrain, leaving the now subdued and only faintly glowing amethyst standing sentinel deep within its mountain hideout.

The track seemed less terrifying to Kirsten on the way down. Even the terrifying Sky Pass had become a welcome mat of fine white pebbles. Her legs no longer twitched at inopportune moments and her muscles contracted with strength and purpose. It was as if she was no longer an individual being, but one with the planet itself.

They were about half way down when they came across Mara's band of marauding Saurians. No longer hidden behind their human disguises but still completely recognisable. Seeing their prey, and only four of them, two elderly and one almost crippled girl, caused them to hiss with delighted anticipation. Kirsten was sure she saw a tongue or two flicking from behind wicked teeth which made her want to gag with revulsion. She could smell them from her high vantage point. That dank smell of rotting vegetation she had had to endure when they had abducted her.

But they were in for a surprise. She was no longer burdened by the weakness of her paralysis. No longer capable of fear. And no longer alone.

With a snarl of her own, she bent slightly and ran down the steep slope straight at them, followed by Gabe's parents, knives drawn while he rose above them all and then dove straight for Mara.

She was quick, and dodged him by rolling behind the large rocks that had tumbled from the mountain and edged the path. He connected instead with her lead henchman and they swirled and fought ferociously. Mara emerged from behind the rock, weapon drawn, ready to fire at Gabe's back. She didn't get the chance to pull the trigger as Kirsten reached her with the speed of a mountain storm. Without thinking, or she would have realised she had no weapon and no fighting skills, Kirsten skidded as she reached Mara, so her feet connected solidly with Mara's, completely knocking her off balance.

The thin lizard woman twisted sinuously to face Kirsten and hissed angrily. She wasn't used to looking up at anyone, let alone someone as small and weak as Kirsten had been. But this wasn't the easy prey she had taken from her home and tossed around like a rag doll. Unexpected strength and resilience met her clawed hand. Caught, gripped and twisted it, until her whole body twisted back and she lay helpless face down in the white dust of the mountain. Her anger and frustration grew and her mouth opened wide to show sharp, pointed fangs.

Kirsten was even more surprised by her own strength. She had not thought past the initial contact with the Saurian leader and now she was not quite sure what to do. It was not in her nature to be aggressive. Her hesitation was enough to give Mara the opportunity to twist out of Kirsten's grip again and break away. Not fully aware of what she was doing, but somehow knowing it was inevitable, Kirsten ran headlong into the other woman. Her momentum drove both of them over the edge and they fell over the edge and into the abyss.

Gabe watched briefly as his opponent's corpse disintegrated into grey ooze and disappeared into the dirt before looking around. His parents were fighting the others, side by side and holding their own but where was Kirsten?

His heart sank as he saw scuffle marks leading to the edge between the boulders. His feet rose from the ground with no conscious thought and he peered into the chasm.

Two figures were falling, hurtling towards the rocky ground beneath. No sound came from either and he feared that Kirsten might be already dead.

He gave chase, his wings beating rapidly to drive him faster than he had ever flown. Wind whipped his hair back and stung his eyes but he was making ground.

Kirsten's whole body tingled with fear as she fell. It was so very far down. She just had enough time to think at least she wouldn't feel the end, unlike the slow death that she had been preparing for. Suddenly, her fall was halted, abruptly but gently, by Gabe's arms around her. Still looking down, she watched Mara hit the ground and explode into slime before she even realised that she was now hovering, gently, above the floor of the canyon.

She turned her face into Gabe's chest and sobbed uncontrollably with relief. She felt his hand threading gently through her hair as he tilted her face towards his and kissed her slowly and tenderly.

She had thought it before, but now she knew that this was it. If her life was concentrated to one moment of perfection, this was it.

Reluctantly, they drew apart, still holding hands, floating. It wasn't over. Constantine and Dokkia where still on the mountain, fighting the others. Gabe pulled Kirsten close again and they flew upwards in long arcs, catching the thermals. But as they crested the rise, expecting a battle, they were met with Gabe's parents, laughing as they looked around at the dark patches surrounding them on the pale pathway. His mum's usually neatly braided hair had tumbled out in a wild silver cloud and she looked younger and more carefree than he had ever seen her. His father looked even more dashing as he slowly wiped and sheathed his knife. Gabe suddenly realised where Cam had gotten his wicked grin from. Who knew?

Gabe tried not to look too shocked. His parents, far from the gloriously kind and just the slightest bit boring façade they presented, were warriors as fierce as any Guardians he had ever met. He felt at once proud and in awe of them. They looked back at him with a reflection of the same pride.

"One battle done," said Constantine with satisfaction, "a thousand more to come." He walked over to a patch of soft grass and spread the tapestry rug over it.

Dokkia nodded in agreement as she followed him and sat down. Withdrawing a carefully wrapped satchel full of her husband's special pastries from Gabe's pack, she said, "we will prepare our people. But first, we will eat!"

Kirsten laughed with happy relief and joined them on the rug. She was so hungry. It was an unaccustomed feeling. After months of not being able to move and always feeling faintly sick, every cell in her body was crying out to be fed.

It turned out to be the most amazing meal in the most beautiful yet impossible setting she had ever beheld. The company was unparalleled too. Family. She could get used to this. For the first time in forever, a faint hope for the future began to stir deep within her heart. Whereas she had been resigned to nothing but suffering and death, now she could imagine sunshine and joy ahead of her.

There was only one planet wide war to finish and she be free to step into the brightness. And, sitting on the rug, thoughtfully chewing a delicious Sweetberry roll washed down with crystal clear mountain spring water, she felt like she could almost taste victory.

CHAPTER 24

Work on the serum was progressing quickly. More quickly than anyone could have hoped for.

The small plants were growing rapidly, every donated leaf regrew two more. Some were already blooming and ready to set seed. Elyse had replanted most of them into an even bigger growing box that she had found in a storeroom and she could almost imagine how good it felt for them to stretch their ever-expanding roots into the gel medium. Warmth and the soft glow of lamps above were so different from the rocky, harsh and wintery mountain of their birth.

It was still too dangerous to open the window shutters and, luckily, the scientists were so absorbed in their work that natural light wasn't much missed. Leaves were carefully harvested, sprinkled with organic residue and the resultant crystals, ready to slash invading parasites into dust when activated, were added to a sterile solution then bottled into vials, ready for distribution. There was a part of the puzzle missing. These crystals weren't merely inert minerals, but what were they? And the reason why they moved was still unclear. Scientists would probably spend a lifetime researching these purple rocks. Everyone knew that they were functioning as technicians at the moment, but also that it was the most important job of their lives.

Elyse kept remembering how Gabe had held Kirsten after she had been injected and how the glow from his eyes had seemed to emanate from him and into her. She also theorised, without being able to prove it, that the light had a significant impact on the effects of the serum. She would have loved to have her hypothesis validated by in situ mass spectrometry, chromatography or isotopic labelling systems, but for now, she would just call it amethyst magic.

She remembered the legend Kirsten had told her about. The legend of Far Mountain opening up allowing beams of light to surround and defeat the enemy. She wondered if Kirsten and Gabe had found the source of the light on their journey and hoped they would be back soon, even though the city was far from safe at the moment.

Talking of magic and amethysts, she hadn't seen Adrian for days. He must be so tired, of fighting the Saurians, of flying night and day, of being one of the few who were now needed the most. As if hearing his name, her Guardian walked through the door. His eyes scanned the room and brightened as he saw her.

Not wanting to show her feelings in front of her colleagues, Elyse settled for a smile as she stood and took his hands in hers. She was right about the fatigue. He looked ready to drop. Without giving him a change to complain, she took charge, making him a fold snack and the strongest coffee she could manage. It bought some of his strength. She began to see the worry his tiredness had masked.

"What's wrong?" she asked.

"It's Cam," he told her quietly. "He and some of the others have been wounded. He is hurt badly. We are not sure if they are infected. So far, they aren't showing any symptoms, but they didn't want to risk passing anything on to you and your fellow scientists because the whole world is relying on you."

She nodded. Even though it was so important that the Guardians were at their full strength, the work on the serum had to continue. There was a growing number of vials but so many more needed to be completed and distributed for their solution to work. But a few had to be spared for the wounded Guardians who were the only protection the world had at the moment.

Elyse left Adrian to talk to her colleagues, who instantly agreed. They would have been already dead if the Guardians had not intervened. A box of vials was quickly packed and handed to Adrian who nodded solemnly as he accepted the offering. Everyone wished their new found friends the best as he turned to go. Elyse walked him to the door, not wanting to say goodbye again. He leant his forehead against hers and closed his eyes. That reminded her of something.

"Adrian, the serum is not enough. It needs the light of the amethyst. We haven't figured out how and why. But the light from your eyes will activate it. Here, let me hold your arm. I will give you a dose so you can see how it's done."

"Good to know" he said, rolling his sleeve up. When it was done, he kissed her cheek, with the softest, briefest touch, before turning away. "I'll return as swiftly as I can. Stay safe."

"You too," she whispered back, but he had already gone. It was time for her to return to her plants. Like small children, growing too quickly, they needed food and water constantly to thrive. With renewed energy she set to preparing the rest of the serum. By morning they would have enough to inoculate the entire population of Harbour City. None of the team would sleep this night. There would be plenty of time for that when their work had been completed.

CHAPTER 25

A drian flew swiftly to the edge of the city where his wounded friends were sheltering in the underpass. He was shocked to see the change in Cam who looked grey and drawn, as if his lifeforce was being extinguished. The gash in his side had changed from a deep red to an ashen colour too and increased in size. Rose was kneeling over him with an unaccustomed look of concern as she pressed a cloth against it. She too had a minor wound, but was ignoring it completely which Adrian thought much more in character from his team mate.

As he approached, she looked up and her expression changed into a carefree smile that didn't look convincing in the slightest. Adrian didn't bother with niceties as he crouched down beside the pair and unrolled the vials from his pack. Without a word, she turned back to Cam just in time to see him losing consciousness.

Rose pushed Cam's sleeve up and held it so Adrian could inject his brother with the serum then tried to wave him away to tend to the others, but Adrian captured her arm and injected her too. She nodded ruefully and sank down beside Cam, her eyes glowing softly. If he wasn't sure his brother was a confirmed bachelor, he would have been sure something was going on between those two.

Possibly, he should have waited to see if there would be any ill effects before treating the rest of the Guardians, but there was no time to waste. He couldn't afford to put any medical staff in danger by involving them. They would be found by the Saurians instantly if they broke cover and without any intervention, they were as good as dead anyway.

As he was completing the injections, he heard Cam coughing. Racing to his brother's side, he witnessed him arching backwards and being thrown about as if by an invisible force, before taking a huge breath and opening his eyes. They were glowing as intensely as Rose's were now. Adrian looked at the rest of the Guardians to see the same glow emanating from them. Cam rubbed at his side before Rose could stop him, but as she looked, she gasped. The wound was healing at an incredible speed.

"So itchy," Cam complained, still trying to scratch.

"Stop being a baby," she chided him. "Mine's itchy too, you don't see me tearing at it, do you?"

Cam frowned at her with an attempt at severity but ended up grinning widely instead. Rose made a sound that sounded suspiciously like a stifled giggle. Adrian looked down at the pair no longer in doubt that they had feelings for each other. He definitely knew how they felt. Wanting to get back to Elyse, but knowing it was not possible yet, he gathered the now recovering Guardians.

"You need to rest now, for as long as it takes to get your strength back. You guys are no use to anyone at half health. I'm going to scout ahead and see what those lizards are up to."

No one tried to stop him. Despite feeling fantastic while lying down, as soon as the wounded Guardians tried to get up, dizziness hit hard. Whatever that serum was doing, it hadn't finished yet.

It was just as well, the heights and depths Adrian would attempt to achieve, he wouldn't want any of his friends to follow. He just wished he could have had even a moment more with Elyse.

Flying skyward, beyond the clouds to where the turquoise sky turned deep teal and the protective gossamer web hung motionless, protecting all that lay below, he spun in the thin air and floated high above the ruins which lay beyond the city. What he had been afraid of was already happening. Looking down, he saw a gaping hole in the centre of the castle from which emerged a dark smudge. A column of Saurians was heading inexorably towards the ocean and Far Mountain beyond. Long shadows fell across the ground as the sun, still brightly orange up here, sank below the horizon.

He waited just a little while longer, then turned and dove towards the ground. With barely a sound, he glided into the castle entrance. It was dark and warm here, dimly lit with torches mounted on the weathered stone walls. Folding his wings silently Adrian landed on the soft dirt surface and crouched into the shadows created by the many arches surrounding the subterranean entrance.

Guardian training had prepared him for the maze of tunnels leading to the Saurian lair. One of his ancestors, long ago, had been captured and dragged down here but had managed to escape. With that escape came the invaluable knowledge of the cave system.

The Guardians had made several attempts to flush out the lizards and rid their planet of the invaders, but had been repulsed and slaughtered at every turn. To be in here was to face certain death. But he had to gather information on their forces. Luckily the tunnels were full of offshoots and dead ends that he could sidestep into whenever he heard the hissing of his enemy approaching.

It took seemingly hours of descent before the tunnel opened up into a cavernous space. The lighting was brighter and reflected off close to fifty Sky-flyers, lined up, facing the back wall. Occasionally the wall disappeared and another flyer would return from night patrol. The incongruous mixture of caves, torches and high tech reflected the character of the invaders perfectly. Even though they could fly, and live in the light, they preferred the inky dampness deep within the planet.

In the centre of the cavern, a beaconing device stood on an elevated platform, facing a small gap in the cave through which starlight shone. A crowd had gathered around it. A nasty chill crept along Adrian's spine at who was speaking from beside the beacon. Mara. Not dead. And neither were any of the other Saurians he and his team had ever vanquished.

Oozing into the depths was not the end for these hideous creatures.

The implications were horrific. They were an unkillable army. A foe that could re-form at will and attack again and again. The only question was why hadn't they? What were they waiting for?

Adrian had to warn the others. He turned to leave, and as he did a tiny rock dislodged from under his shoe and rolled slowly but loudly down towards the gathering. He froze, pressed against the cave wall, hoping they hadn't heard him. But they had. As one they turned to the sound and their yellow eyes narrowed as they hissed angrily when they saw his faint outline. He was unmistakable with broad shoulders and flowing cape. Their enemy, alone, vulnerable and within reach.

Mara motioned to the guards who moved away and gave chase. Without hesitation, Adrian broke cover and ran headlong back along the maze of tunnels. They were so convoluted that he had to use every one of his senses to keep out of the dead-end tunnels designed to deceive and trap. The walls were too close to be able to spread his wings and fly. A blaster flashed beside him and a chunk of cave wall tumbled down, narrowly missing him.

Even though flying came naturally, he hadn't had to run for a long time and his leg muscles began to burn on the ever-upwards path. He heard reptilian claws clicking against the ground behind him as they gained on him. But finally, he was out. In the fresh air, surrounded by the structures of his ancestors. Still running, his wings unfurled and he soared into the starry sky. Grey blast flashes followed and barely missed him as he banked hard.

Then a searing heat tore through his wing, and like a great wounded bird he fell back towards the ground. Thudding face first into the long grasses of the plain surrounding Harbour City, Adrian groaned in frustration. Pain followed as the reality of what had happened flooded his mind. With supreme effort he folded his injured wings back and sheathed them moments before the Saurians were onto him.

A swarm of them attacked from all directions, punching him in the back before rolling him over and dragging him back to their lair like a broken trophy. The pain in his wing, jarring with every rock he was dragged over made Adrian wish for unconsciousness, but as they kicked him finally over the edge of the cavern to land humiliatingly at Mara's feet, he stayed frustratingly awake, feeling the blood dripping from his wound.

Mara smiled with cruel satisfaction as she stood over Adrian's bruised body and dug the toe of her boot into his ribs until the air rushed out of his lungs. He wouldn't give her the satisfaction of seeing the emotion in his dark eyes so he let his eyelids drift closed.

"What have we got here? The hero himself, who thinks he is so much better than us because we can't fly. Well by the time we're all finished with you, bird man, you won't even be able to crawl!" She motioned to her guards who took a seemingly insensate Adrian by the arms and dragged him into the shadows before throwing him into a cage made from jagged animal bones and designed to create fear in anyone locked within its wicked walls.

Adrian lay motionless where he was thrown. In part just to deal with the pain in his wing and mainly so his captors wouldn't realise how alert and awake he really was. It worked. When he did open his eyes carefully, he had been left unguarded.

The cage was small, wider at the base than the top, with a dirt floor and nothing else. He thought perhaps they just let their captives die in here, of thirst. As he turned his head, he saw a small carving on one of the bones, low down, so only a fallen prisoner would see it. It was the shape of a crystal, beams of light radiating from it.

This must be the same prison that an ancestor had been kept in. The same cell he or she had escaped from and gained access to the world above. The thought gave Adrian hope. Rolling over, he crawled carefully over to the carving and ran his fingers over it. It gave just slightly under his touch. Pulling at it, he felt a click as the carving pulled away from the bone, revealing a hiding place.

Adrian reached inside and withdrew an intricately carved blade, silver with embedded amethyst crystals. It was a Guardian's weapon, but one made long ago, by an ancient craftsman. Left for him by a friend. It fit perfectly into his hand and he felt the hum of power as his fingers wrapped around it.

The bones had been strapped together by strips of animal hide and were no match for the blade. But it would take time to make it out. And even if he could, his flying days were over for now, if not for ever. Would he be in time to warn his people of the invasion heading for Far Mountain, advancing even now in the midnight darkness?

CHAPTER 26

The scientists had finally called it a night. The serum was complete. At first light it would be distributed to the population of Harbour City and Elyse would personally deliver the doses needed by her new friends at Far Mountain.

She sat alone in the great room. A small figure on the large couch. She hugged herself, feeling more alone than she had ever been. Not having someone in her life was easier than waiting for her love to come home. Where was he? The other Guardians had already returned, one by one. Healed by her serum and bursting with happiness at their narrow escape, they shook their heads as she asked for news of Adrian. He had left without them. He had not said goodbye.

She knew in her heart, that only something awful was keeping him away from her. He wasn't dead. Elyse would have felt emptiness, but instead, she felt the angst of foreboding. Part of her wanted to curl into a ball and exclude the world and all its problems but Adrian would not want her to give up just because he wasn't here to hold her hand. He would want her to keep going. To succeed.

To drive the parasites from every single human and to win the invasion.

With that in mind, she dragged a soft rug around her and lay down on the couch. She slept fitfully and woke groggily into a grey dawn. He still had not returned. Exhaustion and dread were her only companions. There was no point in trying to sleep again so she pushed herself up and off the couch and began to get ready for her journey.

By the time she had washed and dressed, the others had turned the great room back into a hive of activity. Fatigue was forgotten in the excitement of the coming day. Time to make history.

CHAPTER 27

Gabe and Kirsten waited impatiently for the Sky Train to roll into Far Mountain station. Elyse was bringing the serum and news of the Guardians who were injured during the latest skirmish with the Saurians. She was one of the first to disembark with a large hover-case in tow. Her features were dimmed by tiredness and worry. Kirsten's sisterly concern overflowed when she saw her friend alone and she embraced her tightly.

Elyse hugged her back, tears prickling the back of her eyes. She hesitated for the longest time before explaining that Adrian was still on a mission. The train journey had been interminable without him but it was even harder now to keep from crying when she was no longer among strangers. She looked at Gabe, who echoed her unease. He knew that nothing could have kept Adrian from being here. The sombre trio set off slowly for the meeting hall, giving Elyse time to gather her emotions.

Her case was packed with vials of serum. She was ready to inoculate the entire population. Whether they had ever come into contact with the parasites or not. Gabe would provide the amethyst light and Kirsten would prepare the doses. Elyse held back a sob as she remembered that it should have been Adrian by her side today. Instead, she had his wonderful brother and her exceptional friend. Looking across the room, Elyse saw Constantine and Dokkia watching them fondly. She was with family, no matter what, and to be able to help Adrian's family and friends, was her gift in his honour.

CHAPTER 28

A drian continued to saw through the straps. Several bones were already freed, but kept neatly in their place in case one of the Saurians returned. As he worked, he noticed that where he should be feeling tired, he felt energetic, where he had felt pain, now there was none. Looking down at the knife, he was surprised to see the crystals glowing ever more brightly. He longed to scratch his wing. It was so itchy. That's what Cam had said. Itchy.

It was the serum that Elyse had given him.

At the time, he had felt nothing, but now that he needed it, it was healing him. He sat back on his heals and took some deep breaths with his eyes closed. Visions of herds of strange antelopes filled his mind. They were real. They were inside him and letting him know that they were repairing his wing.

Relief flooded him and when he opened his eyes again, they illuminated the structure around him. The power in the knife was now flowing through him. With renewed vigour, he sliced at the straps and felt them come away with ease.

When the last one had fallen to the floor of the cavern, he pushed at the wall and it toppled like a pile of sticks. Once free, he tried unfurling his wings. They slid open with a freedom he had never felt and he felt like flying straight into that gap in the ceiling.

But there was something he had to do. The beacon. Not sure if the aliens had already tried to send for reinforcements, Adrian knew that they would try and keep trying until they had. He needed to destroy this entire base. The planetary defence system would block any transmission but he couldn't take any chances. He had no weapons bar the knife, so would have to improvise. A Sky-flyer would make an outstanding battering ram.

Crouching low, he made his way silently to the first Flyer and climbed up into it. He had never had the need to use a machine to fly, but as a boy had been obsessed with any mechanical device his people avoided. Finding a crashed Flyer, buried into the side of Far Mountain, he had used it as his headquarters, poring over every detail and playing with every switch until he knew its function as well as a pilot.

But flying a working ship was quite unlike pretending to as a ten-year-old. It was heavy and awkward and moved with a clumsiness that anyone with wings would have found amusing. Adrian was simply exhilarated to be able to get it off the ground.

As the sound of the engine echoed in the cavern, Saurians awoke and ran towards him. Keeping the nose pointing directly at the beacon, he drove the machine into it until it toppled from its platform and broke apart. Guessing the arrow shaped controls were the weapons, he pressed them down and watched grey blaster fire obliterate the beacon. Swinging the Flyer around in an arc, he continued to fire, if only to slow the swarming Saurians while he made his escape. Saying farewell to his childhood headquarters, he climbed out of the machine while it was still firing and spinning and flew straight up and out of the cavern into the bright orange morning sunshine.

He was so late. Elyse would have been frantic, waiting for him. He hoped she had finished her work and left without him. Her task was too great to delay just for him. He arrived at his apartment as the sun reached its highest peak. It was deserted. The serum was gone too. On the kitchen counter a plate of fruit and fold snacks waited for him with a note from her. He smiled at her thoughtfulness. She had done the right thing and left for Far Mountain.

He had not rested for days but felt an unnatural energy, so after eating and washing, Adrian climbed to the roof, ready to fly across the ocean. Headed for home. A vision of Elyse in front of him made him realise that now, she was his home. But there was something else. The mountain itself was calling him. Loudly, insistently. He pulled the knife from its scabbard and saw the amethysts, not just glowing, but vibrating now. There was no time to waste.

CHAPTER 29

The last dose had been distributed. Every Far Mountainer was now protected from the parasites. It was a very good feeling. Word from her Harbour City colleagues confirmed that they too had completed the mass immunisation and were travelling to the other four cities. At times like these, the wisdom of keeping the populations contained to a small area made so much sense.

The trio emerged into the late afternoon sunshine and stretched after being crouched for so long.

It had been a long day, and they longed for some Sweetberry pie and some of Constantine's coffee. It was never too late for a good coffee, Elyse thought. She remembered how mysterious and handsome Adrian had looked the first time she had tasted Far Mountain coffee. For a long moment she closed her eyes against the sun and allowed the memory to hit as hard as it could.

With her eyes closed she felt, rather than heard a thunder beneath her feet. It was like the ground itself was swelling then shrinking. She looked at the others and saw that they too could feel it. On the outskirts of town, a plume of smoke spiralled upwards and the thunder approached.

Elyse's heart sank. It had to be them. The Saurians. They had not wasted any time. As soon as they knew that the population was no longer weakened by the plague, they had attacked. And she had no defence against them. Neither did most of the towns people. Only the Guardians carried weapons, and had the knowledge to use them.

She berated herself mentally for never learning how to fight. No one at Harbour City had. They had just lived peacefully, enjoying science and art and engineering. Never thinking that this life could be taken away by force. Or choosing not to think about it.

The plume was growing nearer. People had gathered around her, watching it. Probably thinking the same thoughts. Dokkia and Constantine were nowhere to be seen and neither were the Guardians. She noticed that Kirsten stood alone, so she went over to the other girl and wrapped an arm around her shoulders.

Before long a column of Saurians became visible at the end of the street. Their grey and ugly forms looked so alien against the sunshine and flowers surrounding them. They were more terrifying than she had even imagined. Even the way they moved was unnatural and disturbing.

Elyse felt an urge to flee but knew it was pointless, so she just stood, with the others, and awaited her fate.

Just as she thought it couldn't get any worse, small plumes of smoke emerged from the ground all around them. And following up through the smoke were more Saurians. These dressed more like humans even though their yellow eyes and the hissing sound they made gave away their evil intent.

Kirsten recoiled and gasped beside her. Following her gaze, Elyse was stunned to see what had to be Mara herself emerging from the smoke. Taller than the rest, her short hair was slicked sideways and a snarl was fixed on her thin face. As she opened her mouth a forked tongue flicked out and tasted the fear in the air.

"But you're dead!" Kirsten shouted, panic in her voice.

"We all are," hissed Mara. "Thanks to you and your little bird friends. And soon you will be dead too, but not like us. You'll be dead forever."

With that, the column of Saurians split in two and surrounded the townspeople then started to constrict the circle they had formed.

Elyse could smell the dank mustiness surrounding her, coming ever closer but she lifted her chin up. Let them come. She had always been prepared to die for what she believed in. And without Adrian, she was as good as dead inside anyway.

She gazed at the deep turquoise sky, wanting the last thing she saw to be beauty and peace.

And as she looked up and beyond the enemy, she saw Adrian. High in the air. A violet glow surrounding him. He was too far away but she was sure he could see her too. He didn't stop, but flew past the scene of impending carnage and straight for Far Mountain, which towered silently above them all.

Adrian never slowed as he neared the peak, he just vanished right into the side of the mountain. Elyse looked around but no one else had seen him. Seconds later the summit above the snow line began to shake. The slopes became steeper and steeper and started to split away from the inner core. Flurries of snow slid down the sides. With the snow, guardians appeared far above them, swirling downwards in attack formation led by Constantine.

Elyse had eyes only for Adrian. He dove from the mountain, completely ignoring the enemy and landed straight by her side, wrapping his wing protectively around her and Kirsten's shoulders as he drew the ancient knife from its scabbard. As one they looked up at the thundering slopes.

Intensely strong violet light beamed upwards from the mountain and touched the sky before jagging down, straight down then formed a shimmering circle around the townspeople. Any Saurians who were under the beam shrieked in agony as they were vapourised while others clashed with the Guardians who plunged, then slammed into their prey like hawks.

Kirsten watched Mara who snarled angrily as she and the remnants of her team advanced, inside the circle, towards her. Despite the shelter of Adrian's wing and the tightness of Elyse's grasp, she trembled. There was no escape. But she felt no fear. The strength of Far Mountain filled her mind and Gabe's love filled her heart. She closed her eyes and stood tall.

Mara lunged, her arms stretching and lengthening, screeching and hissing menacingly.

Her threats were still echoing in the mountain valley when they turned to screams, then silence. Kirsten opened her eyes. Gabe stood before her, surrounded by light, his knife glittering in his hand. Mara was just gone. Kirsten ran into his arms as the light hummed and swirled around them. The fierce battle continued as Guardians and Saurians clashed, but they were lost in each other's eyes. Never to be apart again.

The rest of the reptilians fell quickly without their leader. This time they would not regroup. There was no escaping ooze. The beam had vapourised most, the Guardians had turned the rest to ash which lay on the pale ground beneath their feet, at one with the planet for the first time.

Elyse and Adrian looked at each other with joy and relief. The other Guardians had landed, to be surrounded by the incredibly relieved and happy townspeople. Kirsten's storybook was being relived in front of her.

The war had started. Across the ocean, Harbour City was facing off against an enemy the like of which they had never even imagined. But here, sheltered by Far Mountain, a small battle had been won.

Elyse continued to stare at the mountain while gentle violet light lifted from the horizon and filled the turquoise sky with glorious colour before fading slowly from view. She knew she would never see anything this magnificent again.

As soon as she had that thought, she knew she was wrong, because Adrian was smiling at her, his eyes never leaving hers.

He...was the most magnificent sight she would ever see. A million planets would not compare to this one man. Her Amethyst Guardian.

THE END

Acknowledgements

First and foremost, I would like to thank my own Guardian, Peter, for his unending love and support in the quest that leaves me too preoccupied for reality as I climb Far Mountain.

I couldn't find my vision anywhere, so taught myself how to become AI illustrator with the help of Leonardo AI and Book Brush. Thank you to the people who work there.

So many thanks to my three handsome sons, each adventuring in his own way, showing me the path less travelled and helping this manuscript become a book.

Laura and Ellie - your caring, courage, beauty and intelligence inspired me to create the women in this book.

Isla, Archer, Oliver and Piper, this one's for you.

The Toowoomba Library, where I learned to dream as I lived in the worlds of Andre Norton, Piers Anthony and all the others.

And finally...thank you Elly and Shelby...for your companionship through this journey.

175